ABSOLUTE

TREASON

(A JAKE MERCER POLITICAL THRILLER—BOOK 5)

JACK MARS

Jack Mars

Jack Mars is the USA Today bestselling author of the LUKE STONE thriller series, which includes seven books. He is also the author of the new FORGING OF LUKE STONE prequel series, comprising six books; of the AGENT ZERO spy thriller series, comprising twelve books; of the TROY STARK thriller series, comprising eight books; of the SPY GAME thriller series, comprising ten books; of the JAKE MERCER thriller series, comprising seven books (and counting); of the TYLER WOLF thriller series, comprising seven books (and counting); and of the new LARA KING thriller series, comprising seven books (and counting).

Jack loves to hear from you, so please feel free to visit www.Jackmarsauthor.com to join the email list, receive a free book, receive free giveaways, connect on Facebook and Twitter, and stay in touch!

BOOKS BY JACK MARS

LARA KING THRILLER SERIES
ASSET ONE (Book #1)
ASSET TWO (Book #2)
ASSET THREE (Book #3)
ASSET FOUR (Book #4)
ASSET FIVE (Book #5)
ASSET SIX (Book #6)
ASSET SEVEN (Book #7)

TYLER WOLF THRILLER SERIES
DOUBLE AGENT (Book #1)
DOUBLE CROSS (Book #2)
DOUBLE ASSET (Book #3)
DOUBLE DOCTRINE (Book #4)
DOUBLE JEOPARDY (Book #5)
DOUBLE THREAT (Book #6)
DOUBLE TARGET (Book #7)

JAKE MERCER THRILLER SERIES
ABSOLUTE THREAT (Book #1)
ABSOLUTE DAMAGE (Book #2)
ABSOLUTE FORCE (Book #3)
ABSOLUTE PERIL (Book #4)
ABSOLUTE TREASON (Book #5)
ABSOLUTE VENGEANCE (Book #6)
ABSOLUTE TARGET (Book #7)

THE SPY GAME
TARGET ONE (Book #1)
TARGET TWO (Book #2)
TARGET THREE (Book #3)
TARGET FOUR (Book #4)
TARGET FIVE (Book #5)
TARGET SIX (Book #6)
TARGET SEVEN (Book #7)
TARGET EIGHT (Book #8)

TARGET NINE (Book #9)
TARGET TEN (Book #10)

TROY STARK THRILLER SERIES
ROGUE FORCE (Book #1)
ROGUE COMMAND (Book #2)
ROGUE TARGET (Book #3)
ROGUE MISSION (Book #4)
ROGUE SHOT (Book #5)
ROGUE STRIKE (Book #6)
ROGUE ORDER (Book #7)
ROGUE ATTACK (Book #8)

LUKE STONE THRILLER SERIES
ANY MEANS NECESSARY (Book #1)
OATH OF OFFICE (Book #2)
SITUATION ROOM (Book #3)
OPPOSE ANY FOE (Book #4)
PRESIDENT ELECT (Book #5)
OUR SACRED HONOR (Book #6)
HOUSE DIVIDED (Book #7)

FORGING OF LUKE STONE PREQUEL SERIES
PRIMARY TARGET (Book #1)
PRIMARY COMMAND (Book #2)
PRIMARY THREAT (Book #3)
PRIMARY GLORY (Book #4)
PRIMARY VALOR (Book #5)
PRIMARY DUTY (Book #6)

AN AGENT ZERO SPY THRILLER SERIES
AGENT ZERO (Book #1)
TARGET ZERO (Book #2)
HUNTING ZERO (Book #3)
TRAPPING ZERO (Book #4)
FILE ZERO (Book #5)
RECALL ZERO (Book #6)
ASSASSIN ZERO (Book #7)
DECOY ZERO (Book #8)
CHASING ZERO (Book #9)

PROLOGUE

"Your move, agent."

Nikolai considered the board for a moment. Or rather, he looked at the board and appeared to be considering it. This game was irrelevant, and in any case, he would win in three moves.

He moved his pawn forward one space. There were chuckles from the spectators. A few of them actually knew why they were laughing, which meant they had the same basic understanding of chess that his opponent did. The others laughed because they saw others laugh and didn't want to appear foolish.

His opponent laughed and took Nikolai's queen with his bishop. "Your mind has slowed down, agent," he said, loudly enough that those gathered around the table could hear. "Old age has caught up with you."

Nikolai was fifty-eight years old, seven years older than his opponent. He was no longer an agent and hadn't been for over thirty years. No one had been a KGB agent for over thirty years. His opponent's use of the title was a clumsy way to insult him and rather embarrassing for a man who was on the cover of this month's *Moscow Monthly*

Nikolai castled, a move his opponent had anticipated. The laughter around the table increased, and Nikolai's opponent chuckled again. "Perhaps you want to simply resign now and save yourself the embarrassment."

Nikolai didn't reply. The next move, his opponent would take his last remaining bishop with his own bishop. Assuming Nikolai didn't make the move he intended, this would leave his opponent two moves from checkmate. But when Nikolai moved his knight to the unoccupied space, it would checkmate his opponent, whose meager knowledge of offense was even greater than his appalling lack of defense.

If only Nikolai's true opponent was as foolish as the one who sat in front of him now.

The real problem in front of him was concerning, not because it was particularly difficult to work out a solution but because that solution required many things to go right and could suffer only a very few to go

1

wrong. Nikolai did not like such situations. He preferred to have many avenues of success and many avenues of escape should success become impossible.

His opponent shook his head and took the bishop. "You lose in two, agent. Really, I thought a mind like yours would present a greater challenge, even addled with age. I'm sorry to see you've fallen so far."

Escape was not so important this time. He always planned to die for his country. He would sacrifice himself to save the fatherland if he needed to.

The problem was how to achieve success. How to put his opponent in checkmate and not simply check. This time, Nikolai thought he had it. It had taken most of his life, but he had worked out every detail, anticipated every move, learned everything about the game, the pieces and the opponent to know how they would react to every decision he made.

This time, he would succeed.

He moved his knight. "Checkmate."

The spectators fell silent. His opponent stared in shock. A moment later, Nikolai knew, he would overturn the board in frustration and loudly accuse Nikolai of cheating, a claim he could not prove and wouldn't dare to try even if he could.

Normally, Nikolai would endure such outbursts, but today, he had real work to do. He stood and patted his opponent's shoulder. "Good game, my friend."

The clattering of the overturned pieces sang in his ears as he left the bar. His opponent screamed and shouted and allowed two of the spectators to hold him back, a childish tantrum but one that insecure men always threw.

He didn't look back as he left. This was only a diversion. The real game had begun.

And like this game, it would end leaving his opponent nowhere to go.

CHAPTER ONE

"What an excellent idea," Senior Special Agent Jake Mercer of the Secret Service grumbled as he scanned the growing crowd on the White House South Lawn. "What better way to celebrate the State of the Union than allowing thousands of strangers onto the front lawn of the damned White House?"

The President had decided to make this year's State of the Union Address special by inviting people to observe it live on the South Lawn. Not just the press, although the press got to stand closest behind a cordon of Secret Service agents and in front of a line of hand-picked bodyguards.

No, he was allowing just anyone to show up. It was limited to first come, first serve, but that still meant that thousands of people were crammed onto the lawn. Who knows how many of them were carrying weapons?

"At least it's not in the Mall this time," his partner, Special Agent Jess Foster said.

"That's not helpful."

Last year, the President had given a Memorial Day speech at the Lincoln Memorial in front of a larger but similarly packed crowd. That year, terrorists had set off a bomb that killed six civilians, and, if not for Jake's timely intervention, would have killed the President.

And here they were, doing the same damned thing all over again.

"Sure it is. This is a smaller space. Fewer places to watch."

"There's buildings with perfect angles for snipers, a much clearer and easier path to the President, and a much higher body count if something does happen."

"And there's a National Guard contingent, Army helicopter patrols, Marine counter snipers, two bomb squads, and an honest-to-God tank here protecting him."

"It's a Bradley fighting vehicle, not a tank. And there's no ammunition in it. It's here for show."

Jess sighed. "Well, I guess we should just shoot him ourselves since it's so hopeless."

"Dammit, Jess! Don't say that on an official channel, even as a joke."

"All right, God! Relax, Jake. It's going to be okay."

"I really hate those words."

"Come on. Bard hasn't tried anything in six months. Do you really think he's going to make his way back onto the scene by attacking the most obvious target at the most obvious time in the most obvious place? Give him credit for some intelligence."

Jake rubbed his temples. "You're giving me a migraine, Jess."

"You're giving yourself a migraine. I'll tell you what. If the President is assassinated today, then dinner's on me. If he isn't, then it's on you."

"Will you…" he sighed. "Forget it. How are we looking?"

"Good enough that I don't mind teasing you so shamelessly. We have counter snipers in position at every single building that can see even a corner of the South Lawn. I called your buddy Max and had him recommend me the angriest, most ooh rah jarheads he knew to fill the role. They're literally praying for someone to try something so they get a chance to use their rifles again."

"Okay," he said drily. "Thank you. What about air cover?"

"Are you being ironic, or do you not hear the rotors of the Apache gunship flying overhead? I'm told they're carrying live ammo."

"They aren't. They're not going to fire thirty-millimeter rounds into a crowd of civilians. I mean the police helicopters that can monitor the situation."

She sighed. "You're no fun when you're nervous. Yes, Capitol Police helicopters are on patrol. I'm talking to one of them right now. He says he can see your bald spot growing as we speak."

"Wonderful. And the National Guard?"

"Just as trigger happy as the Marines and stationed at the entrance to the lawn and behind and to either side of the podium. And before you ask, I have a dozen plainclothes agents moving through the crowd reporting everyone who isn't prostrate in front of His Holiness the President. We're *good*, Jake. We've had enough problems. Don't anticipate anymore."

"It's my job to anticipate them."

"Well, don't anticipate the worst."

"It's my job to antici—"

"Then shut the hell up and let *me* be happy! God, did Sheila forget to hug you this morning or something?"

4

Sheila Jackson was Jake's girlfriend. She had moved in with him three months ago. She was also the President's daughter and was currently with her father waiting to walk out with him next to her mother, First Lady Carrie Jackson and the woman who hated Jake more than anything on Earth.

That wasn't fair. She didn't hate him anymore. She just didn't think that Jake's and Sheila's relationship was appropriate. Technically she was right, since it represented a conflict of interest, but Jake had managed to do his job and avoid that conflict of interest.

"Jake? This is Dawson. We're ready to move in five minutes."

"Roger that, Dawson. We are green out here."

"Understood."

Special Agent Dawson was the head of the President's personal security detail, the four agents who were glued to his side at all times. Jake was the Chief of Security and Dawson's supervisor.

He was also tasked with finding and stopping Eli Bard, a former Secret Service agent turned domestic terrorist turned international terrorist who had come closer to accomplishing his stated goal of overthrowing the U.S. government and killing the President more times than Jake liked.

His last attempt had been his least violent but most nearly successful. He had convinced two other Secret Service veterans to betray their country to earn the money they needed to pay for their loved ones' medical care. If those agents had trusted Bard, then the President would be dead already. Fortunately, they knew that Bard was deceptive and concocted a plan to instead kidnap the President and blackmail Bard into keeping his promise.

Their plan was to commandeer Air Force One, something that should have been so impossible as to be laughable. But they had done it with the help of three other terrorists. Jake had succeeded in stopping the traitors and then been forced to fly the stricken jet and land it on Midway Atoll. It was an experience that had earned him celebrity status and the Presidential Medal of Freedom and one he hoped to never experience again.

So, of course, Jess decided to remind him of it. "Hey, do you think they'll let you fly the new jet?"

"No, and I don't want to."

"You don't want to see all the cool new features? I hear it has a bunch of tv screens instead of instruments. Like an infotainment center in a car. You can basically type in commands and let the plane fly itself."

"Maybe you should fly it."

"Hey, you're the experienced pilot here, not me."

"Focus, Jess. One minute to walkout."

To her credit, Jess knew when to turn it off. She switched to a purely professional tone and said, "Roger. Plainclothes agents report all normal. Police air surveillance is active, National Guard is in position, and my cameras are all green. We are a go."

"All right. Dawson, we're ready when you are."

"Thirty seconds, sir."

Jake scanned the crowd one final time. He could pick out the plainclothes agents fairly easily, but that was okay. He had been with the Service for eleven years, so he was trained to spot people like that. The civilians wouldn't have a clue. And if there were any terrorists among them, they wouldn't either.

He noticed nothing out of the ordinary, and managed to relax as the President made his way to the stage flanked by Dawson and three other agents.

Relax slightly, anyway.

The crowd first cheered, then came to a hush when the President took the stand. He looked out over the crowd, his chest swelled with pride, a soft smile on his lips.

"Friends," he said, "To say it's an honor to be able to share this moment with you would be an understatement. So, I'll just say that I'm humbled and thankful to have a chance to share my thoughts on the direction of the United States.

"Over the past fifteen months, this nation has endured the worst crises to face our nation since the attacks of September eleventh, 2001. We have seen the worst that humanity has to show. And we have seen the best. Thanks to the efforts of brave citizens in the Secret Service, the United States' Armed Forces, the FBI, Capitol Police, Washington Police, and thanks to brave agents of our allies' police and armed forces, we have shown time and again that no terrorist organization on Earth will ever stand in the way of democracy."

The speech continued in the same vein, and Jake couldn't stifle a smile. As Presidents went, Bryan Jackson was one of the better ones, but Jake had spent enough time around politicians to know that even the good ones rarely got anything useful done. It was all a chess game that was focused more on maintaining the status quo than enacting any kind of meaningful change, and the President, like the king in chess, was very limited in his power. Which was probably a good thing. Kings tended to be rather damaging to the countries they ruled.

They managed to make it six minutes into the address before a problem surfaced. "Jake," Jess's voice said, tension replacing her earlier jovial tone. "Ten feet from the left cordon about twenty yards deep into the crowd, seventy from the President."

Jake's eyes immediately flew to the area in question. He picked up on a very nervous looking man in his late twenties fidgeting with a backpack and glancing anxiously at its contents. One of the other attendees glanced his way, and he quickly zipped the pack up and began moving closer to the President.

"Carter, Teller, block his way and hold him for me."

Jake quickly moved through the crowd. Two of the plainclothes agents stopped the man and began talking to him. The young man grinned nervously but made no attempt to push past the agents.

Jake reached him a minute later. He put a hand on the man's back, and the spectator jumped. Jake kept a smile on his face, but his eyes were hard. He leaned in and flashed his badge. "Don't move and don't cause a scene. We're going to check your backpack."

"Oh," the man said. "All right. That's fine. Are you Secret Service?"

"Yep."

Jake unzipped the backpack, and the young man said, "Sorry. I ran this through the bag check at the front, but I forgot I still had my bottle opener in there. That's probably what they detected."

"We'll see."

Jake reached into the pack and pulled out a spiral-bound notebook with about fifty pages.

"Um, those are just letters."

"Mmhmm," Jake said, handing the notebook to Teller, who began flipping through the pages.

Jake reached in again and pulled out a souvenir, a picture of the White House engraved on a shot glass. They sold the trinkets for $5.79 in the White House gift shop.

He pulled out another souvenir, this one a coaster with an image of the American flag under enamel.

There was a small booklet of famous quotes from each President. Bryan's would be either "Never fear the dark, for it will always retreat when faced with light" or "The only thing more powerful than the resolve of the American people is the justice of the American cause."

There were three postcards, a small geode from the Smithsonian gift shop, and a picture of the young man as a much younger child taking a picture with George W. Bush.

And nothing else.

"I like Presidents," the young man said sheepishly. "I met George W. Bush when I was a kid, and he said I'd be President someday. I won't. I'm too nervous, and I went to school for accounting, not political science, but I still like meeting each one if I can."

Jake sighed. "Okay. Well, do me a favor and hang out here, okay? I'll talk to the President and see if you can visit him for a moment after the address, but I don't want anyone approaching him now."

"Okay. Sorry. I didn't mean to make you nervous."

"That's all right."

Jake packed the young man's backpack and assigned Carson to stay at his side. He tapped his earpiece and said, "Hey, Jess. False alarm. Just a fan."

"Got it. Well, hey, you never know, he could be a Mark David Chapman type."

"Well, he's got no weapons, and he probably weighs a buck-thirty-five, so I think we'll be okay this time."

"Let's hope all of our alarms are false. Hey, by the way, I'm thinking lobster."

"Lobster? What the hell are you talking about?"

"Lobster. For dinner. It's on you, right? The President is now walking back to the White House perfectly unharmed. I know this great seafood place in Baltimore. It's a bit of a drive, but if you make DeMusio handle the paperwork, we can make it in time for happy hour."

He sighed. "You're incorrigible."

"And expensive. I hope you have a deep wallet."

CHAPTER TWO

"Russia? He wants to go to Russia?"

Jake stared at his boss in amazement. The silver lining to the ordeal aboard Air Force One six months ago was that the President had finally chosen to heed Jake's advice and remain Stateside where Jake could more easily protect him.

And now he wanted to go to the nation that probably hated the United States the most.

Deputy Director Arthur Davis sighed and rubbed his temples. Other than Jess, he was Jake's closest friend in the Service, and like Jess, he never seemed to be as concerned as Jake about the President's safety.

No, that wasn't fair. He was concerned, he was just optimistic.

"Jake, I don't have to tell you that tensions are high between the U.S. and Russia right now."

"That's literally the reason I think this is a bad idea."

"Well, it's happening, and as usual, it doesn't matter whether we approve. Look, the President is under fire for not doing more to address the war in the Ukraine. He's trying to take an active role in mediating the situation."

"Did he tell you all of this?"

"No, but it's not hard to figure out if you watch the news every now and then."

Jake sighed. "So what is it going to be? Another summit?"

"Yes. Russia, the U.S., a few of their allies, a few of ours. The usual mix."

"And the goal is to what? Get Russia to have a change of heart about acting imperialist?"

"Where's all the hate coming from? You're too young to remember the Soviet Union."

"It's not hate; it's just reality. Our ideologies differ too much to find common ground."

"We still have to look like we want to try. Look, I'm not going to argue about it. That decision has nothing to do with our mission. We're going to keep the President safe. Obviously, you and Jess are going. I'll be back here, but I'll have my phone on twenty-four-seven if you need anything. Dawson and his team are going. You and I are going to review the itinerary, discuss possible threats and our responses to them and handpick a team we both feel safe with."

"Is that even possible?"

"We have to do it anyway. I know you're upset about Trent and Merrill. I am, too. But they're the exception—the very rare exception—not the rule. Most of the agents here would immediately die for the President if they had to. You and I are doing this mostly for our peace of mind but also to ensure that we're on the same page and prepared for anything we might face."

"Why is it just you and me? Jess should be here."

"Jess is poring over the new Air Force One with a fine-toothed comb and a busload of Air Force inspectors. They would prefer to handle the preflight inspections from now on. Can't say I blame them."

Trent and Merrill were the two agents that had betrayed the President and tried to kidnap him and his family. They had somehow managed to sneak multiple bombs on board the plane. Needless to say, despite Jake's heroics, the Air Force wasn't very happy with the Secret Service after that.

"So why is Jess there?"

"I think she's dating one of them."

"Ah. Gotcha."

"Don't start saying anything about conflict of interest, Jake. We all know about your little indiscretion."

"She's not an indiscretion, she's my girlfriend. And I didn't say anything."

"I saw the frown."

"That's just my face."

"Well, turn that face to this here," Art turned a map of Moscow around, "and tell me how we make this safe."

"Airstrikes."

"Funny. Now look at this map and help me out."

The map showed alternate routes from the airport to the hotel where the President would be staying and alternate routes from that hotel to the Kremlin, where the summit would take place. Jake studied the map for potential threats and came to the unsurprising conclusion that it didn't matter which routes he chose. All carried a potential for a sniper, a gunman, a bomb, or some off-the-wall Trident play that no one could see coming.

Trident was Bard's organization. Before he took it over, it was a loose gathering of dissidents. Under his leadership, it had briefly become the largest and most powerful terrorist organization in the world before Bard's overreach and poor choice of friends had greatly weakened the group.

Still, Bard was incredibly resourceful and capable of quickly recruiting people to his cause, so Jake wouldn't be surprised if he resurfaced in Moscow. Especially in Moscow. Anti-American sentiment in Eastern Europe was at its highest since the Cold War, and while Russia was no longer the Soviet Union, it was still the leader of that side of the globe. Where it went other countries followed, and right now, it went a decidedly anti-Western direction.

"We'll take this one," Jake said, pointing at the green highlighted route from the airport to the hotel, "And this one," pointing at the red highlighted route to the Kremlin. "Those are the fastest routes, and they limit the possible threats to a few thousand or so."

Art chuckled and this time didn't comment on Jake's attitude. "Yeah, I figured as much. Now about protection. It's a dream to think we're going to be allowed any kind of air support, even drones. It's a pipe dream to think we'll be allowed to look at anything without some Kremlin agent ensuring we don't see anything. I've reached out to my contacts in the CIA, and they have assets that can scope out the Kremlin, the airport and the hotel before we arrive, but there's not going to be any chance of real-time information. Also, we've been asked to limit the President's protection to a dozen agents."

"And we told them to shove it up their asses, right?"

Art sighed. "Well, from what the White House has told me, they've bargained it up to two dozen agents, but that's the best we're going to get."

"I can work with that number. Dawson and his boys are a shoo in for the detail, obviously. Jess handles communications and logistics. She can have two people to help her. That's eight so far."

"You'll want some agents for the First Lady and the First Daughter," Art informed him.

"What?"

"They're going too."

Jake blinked. "Is it even worth asking why?"

"The President wants to show that he trusts Russia."

"Why the hell would he trust Russia? They haven't done anything to earn our trust."

"I can't imagine they'll be stupid enough to let anything happen to the First Family."

"Did he not learn his lesson in France?"

"I don't know. Why don't you go ask him?"

Jake sighed. He knew better than anyone that when Bryan had his mind set on something, changing his mind was impossible.

"Okay. Then I want two agents each on Carrie and Sheila, and RRT Two to provide heavy firepower."

"We can't have people in battle dress uniforms in the middle of Moscow."

"They'll wear standard-issue black uniforms instead, but their weapon loadout remains the same. We might need to ask for forgiveness and not permission, but this is important, Art. If something does happen, and we need to fight our way out, these guys are going to have a much easier time of it then ordinary agents will."

Art sighed. "All right. I'll talk to Munoz. That's twenty-four, and it leaves us no one to guard Air Force One."

"That's another ask for forgiveness. The Air Force will handle the plane's security. They can assign as many service members as they deem necessary, and we'll claim that we thought that since they're staying with the plane, they didn't count as part of the President's protection."

"You realize it's the President who will have to explain these diplomatic faux pas' right?"

"I realize that we need to keep him safe in the most dangerous country to keep him safe. He'll have to just accept the situation."

Art shook his head. "I still can't get used to how easily you talk about him like that. I know he's your friend, but damn."

"That's the job. Safety first, even if that means we have to be stern about some things."

"I know. All right. Start naming names."

They spent another hour handpicking agents and assigning them to the various roles that needed to be filled. That task was far harder after Trent's and Merrill's betrayal. If two veteran agents could turn out to be traitors, then Jake didn't know who he could trust at all.

In the end, he picked agents based on seniority, experience in role and personal details like family life. Trent and Merrill both had turned because of family members experiencing health crises, so anyone going through that was out. People in financial difficulties were out too. No one with a compelling reason to risk it all on a hail-Mary shot at salvation.

The team they came up with was solid, but all Secret Service teams were solid. The Service had some of the strictest hiring standards in government, for obvious reasons, and there could be no learning curve for the same obvious reasons.

So things were as good as Jake could expect.

That still wasn't enough to ease his worries.

***

"I still don't understand why we couldn't eat at the restaurant," Jess said, handing Jake a hoagie and a cup of coffee.

"Because we're talking about state secrets," Jake said.

Jess took a seat at her computer and said, "No one at Fred's Hoagies gives a damn about state secrets. They're too busy enjoying perfection."

"And yet you wanted lobster last night."

"I wanted you to buy me an expensive dinner. I'm trying to establish expectations early on in my relationship with Captain Braden. When I tell him that the hero who landed Air Force One on three engines and half a rudder bought me a two-hundred-dollar lobster dinner, he'll have to one-up you, and I'm looking forward to seeing what he comes up with."

"Jesus Christ. You're a nightmare."

"Only to the men I date. Now get on with the state secrets before I take a bite of this cheesesteak and stop caring about anything else."

"Well, I want your thoughts. What do you think we need to worry about next week? I mean, really worry about."

"The hotel."

"You think so?"

"Yes. The Kremlin is a heavily guarded building, even more so than the U.S. Capitol. Even to kill the U.S. President, Russia will take an attack in that building very poorly, and it would be next to impossible to make it happen. Yes, I know that Bard has done next to impossible stuff before, but I think it's a stretch to say he could do it in Moscow.

"The airport serves a lot of civilian passengers, but like all airports, it has extreme security. Getting a weapon through would be difficult. It's possible, but not likely.

13

"The hotel, on the other hand, serves civilians year-round and doesn't have year-round security. It will have security during the summit, but there are a lot of days before the summit where someone could arrange for things to be where they should be—or shouldn't be, depending on how you look at it—before anyone's looking. If Bard is trying anything, I think it will happen at the hotel."

"You don't think he'll try to take out the Russian President along with ours?"

"I don't think so. He hasn't even managed to take ours out yet, and he's gotta be feeling pretty humiliated by now."

"Humiliated people are sometimes crazy people. Crazy people try crazy things."

"Well, let's hope he does try something crazy, because it might allow us to catch him this time."

"No, he won't be there. He'll be working through someone else like he always does."

"Between you and me, I don't think he'll be working at all. I think we might be focusing too much on Trident."

"Who should we be focusing on?"

"Someone else. Like you said, Russia doesn't like us. I think it's a mistake to hunt for bombs and let someone stab us in the back. I think we need to worry about some ordinary Russian citizen deciding this is their chance to make history."

Jake frowned. Jess raised a good point. He had been so focused on Trident that he had forgotten that other, more mundane threats existed as well.

Things would be so much simpler if the President just stayed home.

CHAPTER THREE

Jake took a seat at the bar, and when Kiana saw him, she brightened. "Jake! How are you? I haven't seen you in forever!"

After dinner, Jake had started home, but his thoughts were still all over the place, and he didn't want to annoy Sheila. The two of them enjoyed a nearly perfect relationship, but Sheila had made it clear that she didn't want Jake bringing work home. She wasn't exactly in love with her father's political career and had made it very clear that she couldn't wait for it to end so she didn't have to be a public figure anymore.

She and Jake hadn't discussed what would happen with them once her father retired, but Jake knew that Sheila hoped he would retire, and they could move somewhere quiet and live a simple life. Jake wasn't sure he could do that, and Sheila knew he wasn't sure. Rather than address that issue now, though, she had simply made a rule that they wouldn't talk about the Secret Service, her father, or Jake's assignments at home.

So he didn't go home. Instead, he texted Sheila that he would be out late and rode to The Sniper's Nest, a bar in Falls Church, Virginia, a nearby suburb owned by Jake's friend and former mentor in the Marine Corps, Max Harrison.

The bar was busy when he arrived. It was always busy. Aside from a great rustic aesthetic that appealed to a wide range of patrons, Max's niece was the bartender and among the most physically attractive women Jake had ever seen. Plenty of men visited regularly out of hope that she might look their way one of these days, and plenty others visited with no expectation of ever getting anything but jut enjoyed the view.

And the rest showed up because the drinks and food were top notch. Max would never be a Michelin Star chef, but he knew how to cook a cheeseburger. Jake smiled at Kiana. "Hey, kid. How's school?"

"Stressful as hell, and I hate my professor, but what else is new? Against all odds, it looks like I'll get my thesis done in time, so as long as Stuffy McStickUpHisButt doesn't trash it just to be an asshole, I should be done with studying for good in about five months."

"All that just to earn the right to study some more for the rest of your life."

"Research is different from study," she corrected. "I get to choose what I want to study when it's research."

"Good point."

A few more customers walked in, and Kiana sighed. "Ugh! Duty calls. Cask bourbon and a patty melt on rye?"

"You're an angel. And if you're uncle's here, tell him some guy just said the Army has it all over the Corps, and he should probably come have a word with him."

She laughed and shook her head. "I'll tell him something a little more clever than that, how does that sound?"

"You're an angel."

"You said that already."

She left and placed his order, then went to attend to the other customers. A few minutes later, a barrel-chested man in his late fifties with a salt and pepper crew cut and eyes as hard and gray as flint came up to the bar. He carried the most delicious-looking sandwich Jake had ever seen, along with a snifter of even more delicious-looking whiskey.

"I'll thank you not to comment on my niece's ass, Jake," Max said as he handed Jake his patty melt and whiskey.

"Is that what she said? Jesus, I told her to make a bullshit Army joke."

Max grinned. "You should know better. She loves getting you in trouble."

"I feel sorry for her husband."

"Eh, the guy's milquetoast. He's used to feeling like a doormat."

"You don't like him?"

"Hell no. A fresh breeze would knock him off his feet. What's he gonna do if someone mugs Kiana?"

"Is he kind to her?"

"Christ, you sound like my ex-wife." He sighed. "Yeah, he's a good kid. I just always pictured her with a man's man. I guess I'm getting old."

"Getting?"

"Watch your mouth, Staff Sergeant, I'll still take you any day of the week. So what brings you to my lovely business?"

"One part business, one part pleasure."

"Well, let's get the business out of the way now so it doesn't spoil the pleasure. What's going on?"

16

"It's the peace summit in Russia. I'm… well, I'm not happy about it."

"Of course not. Bryan won't be sitting behind eighty tons of reinforced steel and twelve inches of Plexiglas. Why would you be comfortable?"

Jake rolled his eyes. "Ha ha."

Max laughed. "Yeah, I get it. And God knows you've gone through enough trying to keep the crazies away from him. But that's the job you chose. I told you when you went out for the Secret Service that it wouldn't be the walk in the park you thought it would be."

"But it was. For nine and a half years. It's only since Trident that the wheels came off."

Max chuckled again, but there was a trace of sadness in the laughter this time. "The wheels were never on, Jake. As long as civilization has existed, there have been people in power, people not in power, and people who hate the people in power. Sometimes the people who hate the powerful are people in power and sometimes they're people not in power. But there will always be people trying to hurt or kill or depose those in power. There will always be people trying to hurt others, and there will always be people trying to take what they can't or won't earn."

"Jesus, Max, I came here for a drink and a pep talk, not a damned philosophy lecture."

"It is a pep talk. It makes *me* feel better to know that things never really change."

"What if you want things to change?"

"Then you're in for a miserable life."

Jake sighed. "Thanks a million, pal."

Max laughed and it occurred to Jake that all of his friends seemed to delight in Jake's discomfiture. What did that say about him?

"Jake, come on. It's not all bad. The United States is still the safest nation on Earth. People here live better lives than ninety percent of the world. The President is still alive and kicking, as is his family. Trident has put together an impressive string of attempts overshadowed only by their string of utter failures. You've caused those failures."

"It wasn't just me," Jake demurred. "I owe a lot to my team, and especially to Jess."

"Fuck your modesty. Obviously, other people helped. But since you're the only one moping to me for a pep talk, I'm giving it to you. You've put Trident on their back foot. They came out with hundreds of operatives and actually managed to be the first enemy power to storm the White House since the War of 1812. Then they had to hire help from a mad scientist to put most of the world on lockdown while said mad scientist started a viral outbreak in Paris and nearly lost control of that scientist. Then he had to hire an arms dealer to destroy half of the Western Wall and *did* lose control of that arms dealer. Then he had to convince two members of your team to commandeer Air Force One and send another rogue Secret Service Agent to commandeer a CIA signaling station. He needed a rent-a-cause terrorist group to help him with that, and you stopped him again.

"He's gone quiet because he's nearly done. He's lost his mystique. You saw it in the news after the Air Force One incident. Instead of talking about him like the looming nightmare whose shadow darkened Washington, they talked about him like a joke. 'Hey, look at the crackpot terrorist again. Now he's going after Air Force One. What a moron.'

"Obviously, it was more serious than the news made it out to be, but my point is that Bard doesn't have the same force of personality he had before. The shine has rubbed off. Now he's just one of a thousand assholes who have tried to topple the government and looked like idiots doing it.

"He's done, Jake. All you're dealing with now are fumes from a fire that you put out months ago."

"Fumes can still kill people."

"I'm not saying be flippant. I'm just saying be confident. Unless Bard builds a hydrogen bomb and drops it on Washington, nothing he does can be as scary as the virus, right?"

"Thanks for that. Now I'm going to be worried about a nuclear threat."

"Well, if you're that insistent on being a wimp, let me try another tack. Suck it the fuck up, Marine. This is your job. I haven't called you to tell you that you're a disgrace to the Corps, and your girl is probably out looking for a real man to wash the taste of your pathetic shriveled little member out of her mouth, so that means you're doing it well."

Jake grinned. "You ever miss torturing recruits?"

"No, because they all turned out to be basket cases like you. I swear to God, your generation and everyone after it is filled with insecure children."

"Does that make you my daddy?"

Max reached forward and took the glass from Jake. "That's enough whiskey for you tonight. Okay, you got the pep talk, now here's the advice. Bard is not the threat this time. The Soviet Union is."

"I know you're not old enough to be senile," Jake said, "so you know that the Soviet Union doesn't exist. That makes this another philosophical point."

"The Soviet Union still exists in the hearts and minds of everyone in Russia over the age of forty-five. They'll be the ones looking to make a statement. We've been sliding closer and closer to a Cold War the past nine years, and those who want the East to rise up against the West will see this summit as an opportunity to wake the bear. Forget about Bard. Focus on the President. If you do that, you'll be able to respond to any threat you face."

Jake nodded. "Thank you, Max. You're right."

"I'm always right, Staff Sergeant. Now can we talk like friends, or do you need to cry on my shoulder a little more?"

Jake laughed. "No more crying tonight, Master Gunny."

The two of them enjoyed the rest of Jake's visit catching up. Max spent most of the time talking about Kiana and her progress in graduate school. Max had never married, and his niece was the closest he ever came to having a child.

Jake shared a little about his relationship with Sheila. He didn't share his concerns for their future but allowed Max to lecture him a little more about how to prepare for that future. In a way, Max considered Jake a son as much as he considered Kiana a daughter. Jake's relationship with his own family was strained, so he saw Max a little bit as his father too. He'd forgotten how good it was to spend time with the old man.

He left feeling better about the upcoming summit. What Max had said about Bard was true. He was severely crippled now, perhaps unrecoverably so. And if Soviet remnants in Russia wanted to try anything, they would be reminded convincingly why they had lost the Cold War in the first place.

Still, he couldn't allow himself to be too confident. As he'd said before, even fumes could kill.

CHAPTER FOUR

The moment Air Force One touched down, everything became a flurry of motion. Things move seamlessly enough one could be forgiven for assuming that the agents were on autopilot, but nothing about the controlled chaos that occurred was automatic. Much of it was driven by scenarios practiced a thousand times, but a lot of it was unique to their current situation.

In fact, the carefully orchestrated series of steps that got the President from Air Force One to the hotel were so complex only because they had to be in order for Jake to feel comfortable. Every agency in Moscow wanted to be able to claim they aided with security. The FSB, the SBP and Moscow Police all wanted their hat thrown in the ring and all jostled for supremacy when it came to ensuring the security of the American President. Jake's team had to plan every step to ensure the Russian agencies received token credit for involvement but absolutely no chance at surveillance.

That was hard work. CIA operatives working in Moscow had already identified two bugs and three hidden cameras in the hotel, one in the President's room. They'd left one bug and one camera in place to avoid detection, and Art and Jake had agreed that no one in the service outside of him, Jake and Jess would be told to maintain the CIA's cover.

That plan backfired somewhat when one of the Secret Service agents excitedly pointed out the remaining bug. Another said he couldn't believe the Russians would do that. The President said, "Don't be foolish. That's not the Russian government, at least not the people in power. It's an enemy or one of the oligarchs trying to find leverage against them."

That was bull, of course. The answer was rehearsed, and the President played his role perfectly. The bug was removed, but the camera Jake left in the conference room had audio, and Mr. Topaz—Jake's contact in the CIA—assured Jake it was positioned somewhere it wouldn't be noticed by his team. The conference room would serve as the place for disinformation. The President and his family had indicated that they would take their meals in the living room of the suite, which

20

left the dining room open for Jake and Jess to use as an actual base of operations.

Since they were in the conference room, Jake decided to feed a little bit of disinformation to keep the Russians interested. He called Jess over and said, "Jess, have Lajoie go over the suite again. I don't want to come across any more bugs. Make sure he does his job right this time."

Jess put on a good show of looking chagrined. "Yes, sir. Right away."

Jake felt a touch of sympathy for Lajoie. He wasn't in on the "joke," so he would actually feel chastised for missing the bug. Jake hoped the CIA was serious about keeping that camera hidden.

They wouldn't feed too much misinformation. They would give slightly incorrect time frames and, of course, give incorrect details about the President's location during the motorcade.

Jake stuck around long enough to solidify the impression of a strict and slightly overbearing boss, then excused himself to head downstairs to the hotel security room. The head of hotel security was Sergei, a portly, heavily jowled man with small eyes and a flat nose. He showed Jake how to access and review the footage in passable English.

"The cameras watch elevator, hallway and all rooms. We keep them off in bathrooms and bedrooms for privacy, yes?"

Jake nodded. "Thank you." His team had actually disabled the cameras in the hotel room, a fact that Sergei was no doubt aware of.

"I label the files in English and Russian so you can see. This is footage from floor"—he clicked an icon, and an image of the President's floor, revealing Special Agents Cooper and Sarkinian standing outside of the President's door—"this is room"—another icon revealed an image of the living room where the President, the First Lady and Sheila sat on the couch waiting for Dawson and his team to clear the suite—"and this is elevator."

The final icon revealed the interior of the elevator that the President would never set foot on. Jake had already decided that the President would take the stairwell and not risk being trapped in the elevator.

"Releasing state secrets again, Sergei?"

Sergei jumped and turned frightened eyes to an older and very fit man who had just walked into the room.

The newcomer smiled and extended a hand. "Kaspov. *Not* Kasparov. Never played chess in my life. I am the FSB attache to the President, which means I'm the FSB attache to you."

Jake returned the smile and took Kaspov's hand. The Russian's grip was firm but not stifling. "Special Agent Mercer. Good to meet you."

Jake was certain Kaspov was former KGB. The man's attitude was so carefully practiced as to be nearly genuine, but there was no hiding the cold shrewdness in his gaze. It reminded Jake of Mr. Topaz, who even among friends seemed unable to turn off the spy's habit of learning and knowing everything with simply a glance.

Kaspov was a threat. He might not intend to harm the President, but he would be the Russian most likely to learn something he shouldn't.

"So? What do you think?"

Jake's brow furrowed. "About what?"

"About security? Is it up to your standards?"

"No offense, Mr. Kaspov, but nothing's up to my standards unless American agents are handling it."

"Yes, of course. As long as those agents are not traitors."

Kaspov kept an easy smile as he said the words, but his flinty eyes made the intent behind them clear. Jake met the Russian's gaze and debated his response. What he wanted to do was bluntly tell Kaspov to back off and let him do his job, and if there was so much as a whiff of interference, Jake wouldn't hesitate to pull any triggers he needed to keep the President safe.

But Kaspov would only laugh that off, apologize for the joke, and insist he was here to be of help. He was playing a game. He might not be familiar with chess, but spycraft was a different kind of chess, and people like Kaspov were the masters.

God, Jake hated spies. Even American spies frustrated him. Topaz was an exception, but only because he was okay with remaining at arm's length.

Jake, at his core, was an honest person. He believed that integrity was the supreme virtue a person could possess. Spies by their nature had to act dishonestly. That didn't mean they were without integrity, but they had to define integrity differently in order to be effective. Jake just wasn't cut out for that kind of work.

He decided he would fill Mr. Topaz in on the details of his conversation. Let the spy deal with the spy.

"My agents are loyal, Mr. Kaspov," he said simply, "and I'm confident that they will be sufficient to provide the President the security he needs."

"As am I. My role here is not to place FSB agents in the President's hotel. My role is only to provide whatever information and help you require."

"And if I require no help?"

"Then I will indulge in the many wonderful pastimes this hotel has to offer. One day, when tensions between our nations are not so high, you must come as a tourist and enjoy Moscow the way it's meant to be enjoyed. Strife has made people forget just how beautiful Russia is and how welcoming its people. Oh well. If only you and I could make policy decisions. Then there would be no need for all this hate.

"But I digress. I will be in Room 337. It's two floors below your President's room and six rooms to the north. But you can follow the signs. Rest assured of one thing, Special Agent Mercer. It is very much in Russia's best interests that this summit go smoothly, and what is in Russia's best interests is in my best interests. I have no desire to see anything befall your President. Quite the opposite. I understand that you don't trust me, and I understand why you don't trust me, but please don't hesitate to ask for any help you need."

"I won't."

Kaspov nodded and turned to Sergei. He said something in Russian, and the security chief nodded so quickly Jake thought his head was going to fall off. When Kaspov left, Sergei deflated, shoulders sagging. He pulled a handkerchief from his pocket and dabbed sweat from his brow. He noticed Jake's stare and smiled weakly. "They make me nervous," he said, "those FSB types. They'll smile the same handing you a vodka as they do stabbing you in the back."

"Do you think he'll stab me in the back?"

Sergei paled, realizing what he had said. "Oh, no no no. It's as he said. It's in our nation's best interests that this summit go well. The conflicts in Eastern Europe and the Middle East have caused some to worry about a large-scale war. Even the most foolish among us knows how catastrophic that would be."

Jake nodded. "Well, thank you for showing me how to access footage. I'll send some agents downstairs to monitor the security cameras. You're welcome to assign employees here as well. I understand that the President isn't your only guest."

"Of course. Whatever you need to feel comfortable."

There's no prayer of feeling comfortable, Jake didn't say.

He headed upstairs, mulling over the conversation with Kaspov in his mind. The man clearly arrived to take Jake's measure, but to what

23

end? Did he want to see if he could succeed in gathering information? Did he want to get an impression of Jake's competence as the Chief of Security for the President? Was it simply a habit of the former spy to probe at everyone he met, even if he intended to do nothing with the information he gleaned? Whatever his purpose, Jake had a feeling that if trouble came around, Kaspov would be in the thick of it.

He reached the suite and had Jess send one of her agents to security. He assigned Special Agent Poole from his own team to monitor the cameras with Jess's agent. There were garden variety wackos too, and he didn't want any of them near the President either.

He went to sleep early that night. Security was established as much as it could be, and there was nothing left for Jake to do but worry. He could do that on his own time.

He lay awake in bed a while thinking of his new opponent in Kaspov. Jake didn't know much about chess, but he couldn't resist comparing Kaspov to Kasparov. Both men were masters but at a different craft. Kasparov was considered to be one of the best chess players of all time, so good that even someone who knew as little about the game as Jake knew who he was.

Kaspov might only be a run-of-the-mill spy. Jake knew even less about foreign intelligence than he knew about chess. But something about the shrewdness in the man's gaze, the calm with which he carried himself, and the way he acted immediately to throw Jake off balance told Jake that he was dealing with a master.

He nearly closed his eyes, then realized he hadn't called Mr. Topaz yet. He pulled his phone out and sent the CIA operative a text.

FSB agent introduced himself as Kaspov. Probable former KGB. Probably threat.

He sent Mr. Topaz the text, and with that worry finally eased, he closed his eyes and let sleep take him.

CHAPTER FIVE

Jake couldn't say for certain that he was in the midst of a good dream when the phone rang. He recalled only a fleeting impression of a woman's warm embrace, her cool lips pressed to his when the ring woke him.

He rolled out of bed, instantly alert. He'd never had trouble waking up immediately, not since the Corps.

"Mercer."

The voice on the other end was disguised to the point that Jake couldn't even tell if it was male or female.

"Your president is going to be assassinated today. You have to change the itinerary."

Jake frowned. "Who is this?"

"Just keep him at the hotel or switch your itinerary," the voice replied.

"This is a secure line. How did you—"

He heard a tone as the voice on the other end clicked off.

"Damn it."

He grabbed his cell phone and called Jess's encrypted number.

Jess sounded a little groggy when she said, "Jake? What is it?"

"We got a call from an anonymous individual who said the President would be assassinated today. I need you to trace the most recent call to my room phone."

The grogginess in Jess's voice vanished. "On it."

She hung up, and Jake dressed quickly. He replayed the call in his mind and tried to determine how worried he needed to be.

The voice didn't sound gloating or menacing. In fact, as nearly as Jake could tell past whatever the caller was using to disguise his voice, he or she sounded genuinely concerned and more than a little frightened.

Jess called back before Jake could dwell on that further.

"The call came from only four blocks away at an all-night corner store. He probably bought the burner there and dialed right away."

"He or she," Jake corrected.

25

"He," she corrected right back. "I have software to do my listening for me, dummy. Your mystery voice is definitely male."

"Good to know. Anything else?"

"Sending you very blurry footage from the store and a map. Get over there, what are you waiting for?"

The line went dead and even though he felt charged with urgency, he couldn't' help but smile. In addition to being a tech wizard and an outstanding partner, she kept his darker side in check. It didn't matter what the situation was, Jess was always cheerful and bubbly. Sometimes that annoyed Jake, but even when it annoyed him, he appreciated it.

He checked his watch as he left. Six in the morning. That made it ten at night back home. Not that it mattered what time it was back home.

He looked at the route Jess sent him and committed it to memory, just in case. Then he tapped his earpiece. "Jess, can you hear me?"

"Quiet and murky."

"What?"

"It's the opposite of loud and clear."

"What… Jess, can you hear me or not."

"Yes, I can hear you. Jeez, just trying to lighten the mood."

Jake sighed. He really did appreciate Jess's sense of humor, but every now and then it would be nice to get a break from it.

He left the hotel and started for the corner store. The streets in Moscow—at least this part of Moscow—looked like the streets back home. The signs were in Russian, and the cars were of Russian makes with a surprising amount of German luxury models thrown in, but other than that, Jake could have believed he was chasing a lead on the streets of Washington, D.C.

He nearly reached the corner store when he heard sirens. He tapped his earpiece and ducked behind an alley. If a crime was being committed, it would be in Jake's best interests not to be seen nearby. The last thing they needed was some kind of diplomatic scandal because a U.S. agent was "caught" robbing a convenience store. "Jess, what's going on?"

"Moscow Police are responding to a shooting. Looks like someone was shot just outside of the corner store."

Jake frowned. "Our caller, maybe?"

"Maybe. I won't know unless you get closer."

Jake tried to figure out how to do that without being seen, but the sound of movement behind him stopped him. He turned and saw a man's shadow against the wall of a side alley before the figure disappeared. "Hold that thought, Jess. I might have a lead."

"Be careful, Jake!" Jess said.

Jake ran after the shadow and quickly turned down the side alley. He caught a glimpse of the figure turning down another alley and picked up the pace. Whoever this was, he was clearly trying to lose someone, whether that someone was Jake or another person.

Jake rushed to that alley and turned right, getting his first good look at the fleeing subject. The man was running swiftly, clearly from something or someone, probably the cops Jake had heard earlier.

From a distance, it was hard to tell much about the man, but he appeared to be of average height and somewhat stocky build, though clearly that didn't hamper his speed. He wore a long tan trench coat and a fedora pulled low over his head. The outfit screamed spy, which meant that Jake's quarry probably wasn't a spy.

But he could have been the person who issued the warning, or the threat depending on his intent. He could have information Jake needed.

So, Jake continued after him.

The fleeing subject led out of the alley onto a major avenue. The buildings here were still well-maintained, and the roads free of trash. Wherever Jake's suspect was fleeing, he was remaining in the prettier side of the city.

Jake ran after him, slowly but surely catching up. When the man looked behind and saw that Jake was on his tail, he turned right into a building that looked like it used to be a market judging by the interior furnishings.

Jake followed him inside the boarded building, and only his training saved his life. He ducked under the machete swung at his neck and the blade buried itself in the wood behind him. He dove forward and rolled, and when he came to his feet, another thrust—this time from what looked to be a switchblade—narrowly missed his chest.

He reached for his handgun but was forced to abandon that plan when a third person swung a golf club so fast Jake could hear the blade sing in the air. He sprinted to the left and heard footsteps follow.

He turned and saw three attackers pursuing him. One was a thickset man with arms as wide as Jake's legs. He was the one carrying the club. The second was a barrel-chested and stout man, though not so muscular as the first. He was carrying the machete. The third was thin and wiry and carried the switchblade with the grace of a cat.

Jake reached for his weapon and spun around, aiming it at the first attacker, but the man holding the golf club smashes it out of his hand. Jake launched himself forward on the follow through, not only missing the blade but missing another thrust from the switchblade.

Jake sidestepped at the last second, and instead of wrapping his arms around the golf club guy, he grabbed the machete wielder and lifted him off the ground. The big man swung the golf club again, and Jake twisted around, swinging machete wielder so that the golf club collided with the man's head. He stiffened, then slumped in Jake's arms.

Jake dropped him and took advantage of the stunned silence on the others' faces to disarm the smaller one. The man shrieked and tried to pull away, but Jake tripped him, sending him sprawling.

He got exactly three seconds with the switchblade before golf club's next strike hit the switchblade, sending the weapon sprawling. Jake swore and jumped back, shaking the pain out of his hands. He was glad the club had missed his hands, or it would have shattered the bones in both of them. Rather than trying to recover the knife, Jake threw a hard left hook, burying it into the golf club's liver.

His hand connected solidly, but the big guy barely even flinched. He grabbed Jake with one hand and threw the agent over his head across the room.

Jake landed in a roll and came up, grateful that his opponents didn't have any combat training. If they had, then the big guy would have known not to throw Jake and give away his advantage.

The two men approached slowly, realizing they were dealing with someone who wasn't their usual mark. Jake felt a flash of irritation, realizing that he was losing—probably had already lost—the man he was chasing so a couple of two-bit thugs could try to mug him. He almost wished he had cash on him so he could just throw it at them and get back to the task at hand.

Then, it occurred to him that these men might have been hired to slow him down. That would explain why they were still coming after he had proven a more formidable opponent than your typical tourist.

Further speculation would have to wait. Jake dodged another swing from the golf club and drove his knee into the midsection of the former knife-wielder. The man doubled over, gasping, and Jake sent a crashing left hook into the man's jaw. He crumpled, but the delay gave the attacker a chance to swing the club back.

Jake saw the blow coming and knew he wouldn't have time to evade it. So, he caught it with his open palms as he jumped to the side. Even with the force of the blow mitigated that way, it sent shivers through Jake's whole body and stung his hands enough that he knew they were bruised.

The golf club looked uncertain. His companions were down, and this man had just shrugged off a strike that should have killed him. Hell, he had used one of his friends as a shield, and it was likely that if he ever got up again, he would do so missing quite a few brain cells.

Jake lifted his hands placatingly and said, "There's no reason for us to fight. I don't have anything you want."

He had no idea if the thug understood English, but the message was clear enough. The attacker frowned and said something that Jake couldn't understand.

The big man rushed Jake, and Jake ducked out of the way. As he turned, he threw a stiff jab into the man's jaw. The attacker shrugged the blow off as though it were a stiff breeze and not a stiff jab.

Jake dove for his gun, but the attacker moved with shocking speed for his size, and once more, Jake was forced to evade rather than attack. He tapped his earpiece and said, "Jess, can you see me?"

"I can see the little red dot that represents you. Also a little red dot that represents what I'm guessing is a very big man considering the fact that you're still fighting."

"Yeah, think wrestler. I can't reach my gun because"—he ducked another blow—"I'm in a confined space, and this guy's fast for a bull elephant. He sucks at fighting, but I'm basically a ten-year-old to him."

"Did you just call me to say goodbye?"

"I was hoping"—he drove his shoulder into the big man to create space and only just managed to back away before the giant wrapped him up—"that you could send help."

"I can call Moscow Police. Unless you want our agents to start shooting at the Russians, they're the only people who are going to be able to get to you."

Jake sighed. The diplomatic incident he hoped to avoid was going to come anyway.

A flash of light caught his eye, and he turned to see the machete only a few yards from him. "Hold that thought."

He dove for the machete. The big man noticed the weapon and swung his club. Jake rolled up and slashed in an upward arc with the blade. He felt the tip bite into the big man's arm, and the brute dropped his club. He cried out and clutched his arm as he backed away, eyes wide with fright. Jake stood and approached, murder in his eyes.

The intimidation had the effect Jake wanted. The big man lifted his good hand and stammered something in Russian, then turned and ran from the building.

Jake sighed and tossed the machete onto the ground next to its still-prone wielder. He couldn't carry that back to the hotel through the streets of Moscow.

"Never mind," he told Jess. "I found a way out. I'm on my way back to you."

He left the building but stayed in alleys until he heard the sirens fade in the background. Then he entered the main street and made his way quickly back to the hotel. The sun shone bright and warm in the sky, belying the darkness that hung over Jake like a cloud.

Who had called him? Had that person been the shooting victim? Had he been the shooter? Had he been the person who hired those thugs to stop Jake from chasing his suspect? Was he the suspect? Was he none of the above?

Those were questions a spy would love to answer. Jake would much rather they were never questions in the fist place.

Fat chance I'll ever visit Russia as a tourist, Mr. Kaspov. I already hate it here.

CHAPTER SIX

Moscow Police had the streets cleared by the time the Presidential motorcade left the hotel and started for the Kremlin. Jake's mind still reeled with questions, but he was forced to put them aside while his team escorted the President toward the Kremlin.

They took a different route than originally planned, just in case the caller's advice was accurate. Jake spent the entire route tense, expecting an ambush at any second. He wasn't sure if the caller was planning an ambush of his own until he reached the Kremlin without incident and ran into Kaspov.

The Russian Agent waited until the President was safely inside the Kremlin before approaching Jake. "I don't want to alarm you," he told Jake softly, "but my agents encountered an individual who was attempting to invade your President's hotel suite to attempt an assassination earlier this evening."

Jake's eyes narrowed. "Did you arrest the agent?"

"The assassin was not an agent," Kaspov replied smoothly, "simply a dissident. I'm afraid that when my agents attempted to apprehend him, he resisted with force, and we were unable to arrest him. We were forced to terminate."

"Did you happen to terminate him outside of a convenience store on Tsar Nicholas Boulevard?"

"Ah, no. That was a gentleman involved in a domestic dispute with his woman. Evidently, when he was approached by police, he attempted to assault them with a knife. The attacker to whom I'm referring was found lying in wait along the route your President was supposed to take this morning. When the motorcade never arrived, he grew enraged and attempted to storm the hotel instead. I guess it's a good thing you changed your plans without telling anyone." He met Jake's eyes. "I wonder what hunch led you to that change?"

"I make it a habit not to make the President's movements obvious," Jake demurred. "Thank you for taking care of the threat for me."

"Yes." Kaspov looked Jake up and down shrewdly. "Well, in any case, he is here now. No one will attempt anything inside the Kremlin. Not with the Russian President and the leaders of so many nations on both sides of the conflict here as well. Good work, Special Agent. I can see why your President entrusts his safety to you."

He left then, and Jake watched as he made his way to a contingent of uniformed FSB officers. He spoke briefly with the men, and one of them turned a cold gaze to Jake. Jake held the man's eyes until the group left. Then he walked into the Kremlin and resumed his place at the President's side.

***

The first day of the summit was filled with the usual posturing. Each head of state was greeted with pomp and ceremony, but the Russian President was, of course, introduced with greater pomp and ceremony. The visitors were arrayed on either side of a long, ornately carved mahogany table, but the Russian President sat at the head. Directly across from him at the foot of the table was the President of Belarus, perhaps the staunchest Russian ally on Earth, but otherwise an unimportant nation. The purpose was two-fold: to throw a bone to the Belarussian President and to make the U.S. President feel unimportant.

Various indignities continued throughout the day. The Western leaders' lunch was lost, and they were forced to watch their Eastern Bloc opponents eat while they waited for their food. The leaders of the former Soviet states were permitted to speak first on each issue. The Russian President made no attempt to hide his disdain whenever the President or the Prime Minister of Great Britain—another staunch opponent of Russian policy—voiced dissent.

Overall though, it was a typical day one. Nothing was said that hadn't been said a thousand different ways before in a thousand different venues. Nothing in the way of actual progress was made, and the real issues, the ones that the heads of state had flown thousands of miles to meet about, weren't touched on. That would come after the ceremonial insults were done with.

The President returned home without incident. Jake changed the itinerary this time too. He didn't like that Kaspov had approached him at the beginning of the summit to tell him about the attempt on the President's life. Strictly speaking, protocol dictated that he inform Jake of the incident right away, but Jake was already suspicious of the FSB agent, and his suspicions weren't eased by Kaspov pointing out that he was aware of the President's actual itinerary when he should only have known about the false one provided in the conference room over the camera that Jake left behind.

He waited until the President and his family were safe in their room, then met Jess in her room. After the phone call the night before, Jake had decided to move their actual base of operations from the President's dining room to Jess's room. Dawson and his team could handle the President's security, and Kaspov clearly had access to their plans. Jake hoped that by moving things to Jess's room, they could take advantage of Jess's technological expertise to avoid any more listening in.

Once he and Jess were safely away from prying eyes and listening ears, Jake called Art. The deputy director picked up immediately. "Davis."

"Art, it's Jake."

"And Jess!"

"What's going on?"

"Well," Jess said, "the borscht isn't bad, but I'm not much of a vodka girl. Too much of a bite." Jake frowned at Jess, who stuck her tongue out at him and said, "Sorry, I needed to lighten the mood or I'd go insane with two gruff men pronouncing doom and despair."

Art sighed. "Okay. Got it out of your system?"

"For now. The real reason we're calling is because there was an attempt on the President this morning."

"What? Why am I only now hearing about it?"

"Because we didn't know about it until we were already in the Kremlin," Jake said. "An FSB agent was the one who told us."

"FSB? How the hell did they know before you?"

"Well, we actually did know about it beforehand."

"Okay, you two need to start speaking clearly or I'm going to start getting really pissed. What the hell happened?"

We got a phone call from an anonymous source early this morning who said that we need to change the itinerary or the President would be assassinated. We traced the call, but when I went to investigate, Moscow Police had shot someone nearby and had the whole area cordoned off."

"Was that someone your caller?"

"I believe so, but I can't know for sure. The FSB agent, Kaspov, said that it was someone involved in a domestic dispute, but I trust this guy about as far as I can throw you."

33

"Because this situation is serious, I won't call you out for being an asshole, but I will call you out for joking at a time like this. So you get a warning, and I assume you changed the itinerary because the attempt took place without your knowledge."

"Yes. The FSB claims to have stopped someone heading to the hotel."

"And you don't believe them?"

"I believe that they had our actual itinerary rather than the one we fed their camera as misinformation. That's how they were there to either stop the attack or attempt to perpetrate it in the first place. Either way, it's a problem that they knew where the President was going to be."

"Yes, it is. Okay, I'll look into Kaspov for you, but that won't be his real name."

"I sent a message to my CIA contact. I haven't heard anything back yet, but that's typical of him. The CIA aren't the best communicators."

"I'm still going to reach out on my end. I know people old enough to have tangled with the KGB, and this Kaspov guy seems old country. My big concern is who could have gotten him the information unless that who was someone on your team."

Jake and Jess shared a grim look. Art had just vocalized Jake's biggest worry. "That's my concern too."

"Any thoughts?"

Jake shook his head. "You and I handpicked these agents, sir. If one of them is a traitor, then it's as surprising to me as Trent and Merrill were."

Art sighed. "Yeah, that's what I was afraid of. Dammit."

The line went silent for a long moment as Art ruminated. Jess offered Jake a wan smile, but even her bubbly demeanor was strained. They had suffered enough grief as the result of moles in the Secret Service.

"How many people are on Bard's side?" Art said, half to himself. "Christ, it's like he's got half the Service to his cause."

Jake hesitated briefly, then decided to share Max's insight with his boss. "Sir, I don't know that Bard is the one behind this."

"You think it's all the Russians?"

"I think it's all Russians," Jake said. "Whether it's *the* Russians or terrorists who aren't affiliated with Russia, I think that it's possible that we're not dealing with Trident at the moment. Bard's been on his back foot since Paris, and each attempt he makes has gotten more desperate and more easily defeated. Well, maybe not more easily defeated, but you catch my point. He's waning, and I doubt he would be able to establish contacts in the Russian government. If he's involved, it's because they got to him and made him give up information."

"Assuming it's government. If it's terrorists, then it might not be the case that Bard is on their payroll." Art sighed. "Okay, you two are responsible for the President, so stay focused on that. Keep the President's itinerary between you and only release it the minute you start to move. Change plans often and without warning the team. They're good enough to adjust on the fly, and if one of them is feeding Bard or the Russians or the damned Martians information, then they won't be able to do it in real time. I'll dig into things on my end and see if I can figure out what the hell's going on."

"Yes, sir."

"Oh, and Jake?"

"Yes, sir?"

"Buddy up with this Russian guy. Keep your friend's close, but your enemies in stabbing distance."

Jake frowned. The idea of sharing space with the slippery Kaspov didn't appeal to him, but he understood Art's point. The closer they were to Kaspov, the more likely they were to confirm if he was indeed working against them.

And the faster and more effectively they could respond if he was.

"You got it, sir."

Art hung up, and Jess frowned and said, "Goodbye to you, too." She looked up at Jake and said, "Do you really think Bard isn't a part of this?"

"I think it's better if we don't assume that. The Russians are good at intelligence. Very good. They wouldn't need Bard's help to have eyes and ears on us."

"Maybe they wouldn't need a mole either," she pointed out hopefully.

The best Jake could offer in the way of encouragement was, "I hope not."

There was a knock on the door, and both agents jumped. Jake's hand flew to his shoulder holster on instinct, and he called, "Who is it?"

"It's Dawson, sir. I need you to come quickly. Someone tried to poison the President."

CHAPTER SEVEN

Jake and Jess sat at the dining room table, staring at the bottle of vodka in front of them. Next to the bottle was a glass containing two ounces of the clear grain liquor. Special Agent Dawson sat across from them while Josiah Trumbull, the President's personal chef, stood behind him, arms folded across his chest, a furious look on his face.

"I'm so glad I thought to check the vodka," he said. "It's laced with ricin."

"You're sure?" Jake asked.

Trumbull glared at him. "Take a sip and find out."

Dawson cleared his throat. "I tested a drop of it with a kit that detects poison. It's definitely ricin. Very highly concentrated. The bottle contains enough to kill the President, his family, and everyone else on this floor."

"It can't be cooked away either," Trumbull said. He shook with rage. "They were trying to get me to poison the man I cook for!"

"I think they were assuming the President would drink the vodka," Jess pointed out. "This retails for nearly four hundred dollars a bottle."

"It retails for four hundred dollars a bottle in America," Trumbull replied. "Here you can get it for thirty dollars. It is mid-shelf fare at a grocery store. I was going to use it to cook because the thought of using well vodka to make food for the President turns my stomach."

"Not as much as that would have turned your stomach," Jess said. Trumbull glared at her, and she lifted her hand placatingly. "Sorry."

"So now we have someone trying to assassinate the President through violence and someone else trying to assassinate him with poison," Jake said. "Was this bottle here when we arrived?"

Dawson nodded. "We inventoried it, Trumbull and I."

Jake sighed. "Lovely. You'll have to test all of the President's food from now on. I don't know if anything else will be poisoned, but I would imagine that they didn't throw all of their eggs into one bottle."

"I told you to let me bring food for him from home," Trumbull said to Dawson. "We would have avoided this problem and the problem that Russian food is shit." Noticing the uncomfortable looks around the table, he said, "Well it is! They can't grow decent beef to save their

36

lives, their pork is tough and their bread is passable at best. The one thing they do well in a culinary sense is vodka, and now they've poisoned that!" He shook his head. "One of you will have to take me shopping so I can procure good vodka for the President. I *insist* on making him vodka-braised beef before we leave!"

Jake didn't want to have that argument with the irate Trumbull right now, so he only said, "We'll talk about that a little later. Go ahead and make something else for dinner, and we'll see if we can figure out who might have poisoned this bottle."

"Make him what? The whole kitchen is poisoned!"

"Dawson, test the food Chef Trumbull selects. If he can't find anything to serve the President, let me know."

Dawson didn't look pleased at having to keep the angry Trumbull company, but he didn't protest. The two of them left, and Jake turned to Jess. "The plot thickens."

She made a face. "Eww, don't say that."

"Why not?"

"It's so stereotypical. It's like saying, the game's afoot!"

"You know he never actually said that."

"What?"

"Sherlock Holmes. He never said the game's afoot. That was made up after the books were written."

Jess glared at him. "Am I this annoying when I talk in non sequitors?"

"Oh yes. Now you know how it feels."

She sighed. "Jesus, good to know."

"I'm going to talk to hotel management and see if I can figure out who could have poisoned this," Jake said. "You go back to your room and keep an eye on me and another on the security cameras."

The day before, Jess's Agent in the security room and sent the feed directly to Jess's monitors so she could remain abreast of the security situation in real time. Jess nodded and said, "Of course I will."

She smirked, and Jake said, "Don't say it."

So, of course, she said it. "It's elementary, my dear Jake."

Jake sighed and left the President's suite, Jess's laughter echoing behind him.

***

37

The hotel manager was terrified at Jake's questioning, but Jake wasn't sure it was him the manager was so afraid of. To Jake's utter lack of surprise, Kaspov was waiting for him when he reached the ground floor of the hotel.

Jake had informed him of the attack on the President, and the FSB agent reacted with shock that could have been real or could have been practiced. He wondered if there would even be a difference.

"Well, that's not encouraging," Kaspov said. "I assume you will be speaking to hotel management to ask who could be responsible?"

"I will."

"Perfect. I shall accompany you. We'll get to the bottom of this together."

Jake nearly told Kaspov he didn't want the FSB agent present, but he remembered Art's instruction and said, "I welcome your help."

So now the manager of the hotel was literally shaking in his chair, his eyes darting back and forth between the two stone-faced interrogators. "I... I am so sorry. I..." he gulped. "I assure you, we knew nothing of this. I... I will, of course, talk to my employees—"

"No, you won't," Jake said. "I will."

"And I," Kaspov added.

The manager paled and shrank back. "Of... of course. Shall I have them wait for you?"

"You will have everyone who turned over the President's room or was present during or after the turnover wait for me," Jake said. "That includes security, housekeeping, hospitality, room service, maintenance, yourself and any other managers, and any kids who were attending bring your brat to work day."

"Bring your what to work?"

Jake sighed and reminded himself that American sarcasm probably wouldn't land here. "Never mind that part. Just get me everyone who was inside that room during or after the time it was turned over for the President's visit."

"Of course! Um... a few of them are on vacation—"

"Where?" Kaspov interrupted.

"Um... I'm not sure—"

"Become sure. If they're within driving distance of this hotel, they're coming here. If not, I'll have FSB agents interrogate them."

"No," Jake said. "I want to talk to them." *Before your agents "terminate" them.*

Kaspov smiled slightly. "Of course."

Jake turned back to the manager. "So you'll put them on a flight or a train, or a damned"—*no sarcasm*—"Just get them here."

"Of course! Right away, sir!"

He hesitated, looking between the two men. When they didn't move, he swallowed and said, "Right. Of course. I'll... you can wait here, and I'll bring them to my office! One at a time!"

When he left, Kaspov turned to Jake. "You don't trust me."

It wasn't a question. Jake's response wasn't a question either, though he framed it as such. "Do you trust me?"

Kaspov regarded Jake a moment. Then he chuckled but didn't respond.

***

The interrogations turned out to be disappointing. Jake wasn't much of a spy, but he was an excellent interrogator. If anyone had known anything about the poison, then Jake would have been able to tell. But none of the employees had any idea, and to Jake, their terror seemed genuine.

Terror was the right word, too. The FSB was a police force. It wasn't even an investigative agency. Nonetheless, when the employees saw Kaspov, the reaction was one of fear bordering on fright. It reinforced Jake's suspicion that the man was former KGB. People looked at him like the devil incarnate.

That meant that even though Jake felt that the interviewees were telling the truth, he couldn't be sure. They could simply be so frightened of Kaspov that they refused to offer their knowledge.

The final interview was the woman who stocked the room with food. She alone seemed to have no fear, either for Kaspov or Jake. She sat across the desk with a flat expression that communicated pride, boredom and mild contempt.

Jake began. "Do you speak English?"

So far, all the employees had, at least to an extent. This hotel was popular with tourists when it wasn't being used for visiting dignitaries. The old woman didn't reply, but her lip curled in contempt, which suggested to Jake that she did understand him.

That was confirmed a moment later when Kaspov said something in Russian, and the old woman rolled her eyes. "Yes, I understand English. No, I didn't poison your President. No, I don't know who did.

No, I won't consent to a search, although I imagine this pig"—she thrust her chin toward Kaspov—"won't care how I feel on the subject."

"You were searched the moment you walked into the room," Jake said. He regretted the admission immediately when Kaspov looked at him with interest.

The sunglasses Jake wore had a scanning function courtesy of Jess that could detect weapons or contraband on someone's body. It wasn't perfect. It couldn't see plastic or ceramic weapons, and it could see liquids, but it couldn't tell you what kind of liquid.

Still, Jake doubted that the old woman had anything on her. Even if she was the assassin, she wouldn't be foolish enough to bring evidence of her position with her to an interview.

"Where did you purchase the vodka?" Kaspov asked.

"The convenience store around the corner. The one the pigs shot up. The manager asked for top shelf. That bottle was top shelf for a convenience store. I figured the Yankee President wouldn't know the difference."

Jake nodded. "Do you sew, Miss Varyan?"

"Of course I sew. All grandmothers sew."

"So you have needles?"

She stared at him contemptuously. "Ask your question, Yankee. Stop dancing around it like a fool."

Jake smiled coldly. "The poison was inserted by a long needle pushed through the cork. You know anything about that?"

"I know that a syringe is not a needle. Both have sharp points. That is it. But of course, Americans are good at making one thing seem like another."

"Is there any reason you brought that syringe to the President's room?"

"Of course. I tried to poison him."

Jake blinked, stunned by her bluntness. He was so stunned that all he could think to ask was, "Why?"

Varyan chuckled. "Because I hate him. I hate America."

"Did you act on your own?"

"Sure."

Jake leaned forward and looked into her eyes. Her expression remained defiant, but something flickered across it that made Jake unsure if she was telling the truth.

"I think you're lying," he said. "I think someone hired you to kill the President. You might hate him, but I think someone gave you that poison and told you exactly what to do with it."

She spat at him, and he recoiled in disgust. "I don't care what you think! Fuck you, American pig!"

"If you'll permit me, Special Agent," Kaspov said, "I can take Miss Varyan to my precinct. We could have a more thorough conversation with her there."

Jake was about to deny that request when Jess's voice came over his earpiece. "Jake, we received some urgent news. You'll have to cut this short."

He sighed. "Very well, Kaspov. You may take her. If you learn anything, I want to know about it."

"Of course. I'll keep you abreast of anything I discover."

Jake left the defiant old woman and the smug FSB agent in the room. She wasn't going to talk to him, so there was no point in fighting anymore. He would have to hope that Kaspov could get something out of her.

Who would hire an old woman to do his dirty work for him?

Jake didn't know, but he knew one thing. They were looking for a coward.

He knew from experience that cowards were often the most dangerous enemies.

CHAPTER EIGHT

Jake returned to the hotel room to see a flurry of activity, not from his agents but from the President and his two assistants. Carrie and Sheila sat on the couch in between to Secret Service agents and watched, shellshocked, as Bryan paced the room, talking into his phone. His personal assistant and the White House attache compared notes and cast worried glances at him.

Jake could only catch snippets of the conversation, but whatever it was, it had the President worried. Bryan frowned and spoke in curt, commanding tones that indicated a level of frustration Jake had rarely seen.

Jess waved Jake over to the dining room table, where she had her laptop open. Jake sat next to her and read the headline on the screen.

"Just caught this from the Associated Press," Jess said. "They found out twenty minutes after we did."

"Then why did I only find out now?"

"By we, I mean the U.S. in general. I think the White House was the first to hear of it, and they called the President directly. We as in me personally heard it when Dawson called me to tell me that the President was freaking out over the news and asked me to get a hold of you because he didn't want to be the one to interrupt you."

"He could have interrupted me for this."

"This" was the death of the U.S. Ambassador to China. The death itself had occurred the night before but had been kept heavily concealed by Beijing police. The person who leaked it was an anonymous source who claimed they had to sneak into India to release the information.

The ambassador died when his auto-rickshaw burst into flames, engulfing him in the process. The source claimed that the auto-rickshaw had been sabotaged, but Beijing Police were hiding that information.

Jake understood why the President was upset now. The Chinese President was notably absent from this peace conference, and if word got out that an American ambassador in China had been murdered, it could make the peace summit a thousand times more difficult. Public opinion was very much anti-war right now, but when U.S. diplomats started getting killed, that sentiment tended to swing the other way quite quickly.

The incident was probably not related to anything happening in Russia, but it didn't sit well with Jake. Aside from the obvious tragedy of the loss of life was the worry that Bard's past actions, though unsuccessful, could be inspiring other terrorist groups or violent individuals to take action against American politicians. A successful assassination would be throwing kerosene on the fire.

"I don't give a rat's ass how you get it done, Travers, just get it done!"

The President's voice thundered over them, and the name he'd used caused the Secret Service agents to look at each other in consternation. Elizabeth Travers was the Director of the CIA. If the President was talking to her, it was either an order to obtain or conceal information. Knowing Bryan, the former was more likely, but either way, it underscored how serious this situation was.

The President stormed over to the table, and Jake stood. Bryan looked at him but addressed both of them. "This attack was clearly an attempt to stall these peace talks. Just so we're on the same page, they will not be stalled. We're on the cusp of ending this War before it begins in earnest. That's worth risking my life for. Are we clear?"

Jake had no intention of allowing the President to risk his life any more than was absolutely necessary, but now wasn't the time to have that conversation. He nodded and said, "Yes, sir."

"Good. Lana."

The personal assistant jumped and said, "Yes, sir."

"I want condolences sent to Bumgarner's family."

"Yes, sir."

"I also want an emergency session of Congress when I arrive home to discuss the sanctions we'll have to levy against China for this action."

"Of course, sir."

"God*dammit!*"

"Yes, sir."

"Didn't need a response to that one, Lana."

"Yes, sir. Sorry, sir."

The President retreated to his bedroom. Sheila started toward Jake, but Carrie grabbed her shoulder and shook her head. Jake offered Sheila a half-smile, then turned to Jess. He would love nothing more than to get some time alone with Sheila, but he had work to do right now.

"Okay," Jake said. "So this is bad news. China's a big Russian ally, and if they're behind the assassination, then it's akin to declaring war."

"If? How could they not be behind it?"

"I'm still considering the possibility that Bard has masterminded this to try to drive us toward war."

"This won't go to war, though, will it? I mean… that's an extreme response."

"It won't go right to war just from this, no," Jake agreed, "but it could ruin the summit. It could send everyone home with an even larger rift driven between us and Russia. We're sliding backwards right now. We could start falling backwards after this."

Jess shivered, not from cold. "So what do we do?"

Jake tapped his fingers on the table. "Well, I hate to say it, but the President's right this time. We can't leave the summit. If we do that, then we're telling Russia that we're not interested in a peaceful solution. We can't afford to do that right now."

"Do you think the President is in danger?"

"I know he is. But we'll need to find a way to keep him out of danger until the summit is over. Then we can go home and let the pieces fall where they may."

"Who do you think the next target will be?" Jess asked. "Do you think they'll go after any other diplomats?"

Jake thought a moment, then said, "I don't think it's helpful for us to speculate like this. I think we continue to do our jobs to the best of our abilities and worry about things outside of our control on our own time."

Jess bit her lip. "I'm worried that the success in China will inspire whoever's here to try again."

"The Russian government isn't hesitant," Jake replied. "If they're going to make a move, they'll do it regardless of what happens in the rest of the world."

"And if it's not the government? I don't know, Jake, I just feel like the way things have been going, we'll need to just end public appearances."

"We're not going to get the President to bend on the summit," Jake said. "This whole summit was his idea. He's desperate to promote peace in the region. The world is."

"I know," Jess said. "But…"

Jake understood. The President was doing the right thing politically but the wrong thing when it came to his safety. In the past, that would have infuriated Jake, but he'd come to see things from the President's point of view. If he showed a weak hand to the nation's enemies, then those enemies would be encouraged to try again to attack and the potential for catastrophe would increase.

Jake was glad he'd never gotten into politics.

"Here's the plan," Jake said. "We're changing the President's itinerary on a moment's notice, just like Art said. The President goes nowhere without two agents with him, not even the bathroom. His family is under constant surveillance, as is he, and no one enters this floor but the people on it right now, and the two agents in the security room. No housekeeping, no food service, no one at all. The summit continues per the President's discretion, and we make sure that it goes without him being assassinated."

"You make it sound so easy."

"We've done a good job so far."

They spent the next hour informing the rest of the agents of the pertinent changes to the security situation. They kept things brief so they could leave before the hour was too late and allow the First Family to sleep.

Jake and Jess stopped by Jess's office before heading to bed. Jake called Mr. Topaz on his burner phone and when the operative answered, he said, "Mr. Topaz, I have problems. Can you tell me what happened in Beijing?"

"Not much more than you can learn on the news," the CIA operative replied. "I can confirm that it was definitely sabotage, i.e., assassination. As far as who might be responsible, or if the situation with the President has changed at all, I don't have anything. My assets in Moscow report that FSB activity has increased significantly in the past twenty-four hours, but I don't know if that's because of the ambassador to China or if it's because of the poisoned vodka bottle."

Jake sighed. "We need to be ahead of this information, Topaz, not behind it."

"I'm at least as aware of that as you are," Topaz replied, "but not all needs are fulfilled. If you want my advice, I would refrain from allowing the President to use public transportation, even the cars provided by the Russian government. Call the U.S. Embassy and get cars for him."

"I'm not sure if the President will be willing to hear that," Jake replied.

"Doesn't matter. Ask forgiveness, not permission. Just don't let him into anything that isn't U.S. And check the cars too, even if you get them from the embassy. If they can bomb a rickshaw, they can bomb a car."

"So you can't tell me anything at all? What about the caller from earlier today?"

"Male, early twenties, maybe even younger. Genuinely nervous according to my speech patterns guy. The call was made from a cheap burner phone. No idea what model. Not that it matters. You can buy them for fifty bucks a dozen at any convenience store."

"Male, early twenties?" Jake asked.

"Yes."

"So it was a terrorist."

"Not necessarily. Could be a concerned individual not wanting to see his country go to war. Let's face it: it's not bragging to say that if it comes to full-scale conflict, the U.S. takes it every day of the week. Most people would rather not deal with that."

"So we know nothing."

"I told you that already."

Jake sighed and rubbed his temples. "All right. Well, thanks for the heads up. We'll reset here and see if we can survive the next few days."

He hung up, and Jess said, "Jake, I really think we should reconsider staying here. If we go home, we're in control of everything. We can *see* everything."

"We couldn't see Trent and Merrill betraying us."

"That's a low blow, Jake. You know what I mean."

"I know what you mean, but I really don't think it makes a difference. I think the one thing that might make a difference is if we remain unwavering. The big players will make their plays no matter what, but the small players will think twice if we show them how small they really are."

Jake's phone rang. Dawson. He put it on speaker. "Go ahead, Dawson."

"Sir, the President wants to see you in his suite again."

Jake nodded. "I'm on my way. Jess too?"

"Yes. We're having a brainstorming session, and the President wants to be a part of it."

"All right. We're on our way."

46

The two of them headed back to the President's suite. Jake had a feeling he knew what the purpose of this meeting was going to be. So he wasn't surprised when he entered the room and saw the President standing in the living room with Dawson sitting nervously on the couch. "Mr. President," Jake said. "You called for me?"

"Yes. Have a seat, Jake. We're talking about whether or not the summit should continue."

CHAPTER NINE

"Who's arguing that we pull out?" Jake asked.

The President chuckled. "Congress, the Vice President, every political pundit on both sides of the aisle. The general consensus is that I'm an idiot for wanting to stay."

"Well, for what it's worth, sir, I don't think you're an idiot. I think staying is the correct choice."

"I appreciate the support, Jake. However, out of respect for all of the other well-meaning people in Washington, I've agreed to hear opposing arguments. So, whose got some?"

Jess's shoulders tensed. Jake frowned as his partner slowly, tentatively, raised her hand.

Bryan lifted his eyebrows. "Jess? You're not with your partner on this?"

Jess sighed. "No, Mr. President. I respect Jake a lot, and normally, he and I would see eye to eye about something this important. In fact, normally, he'd be advocating for a return home the way I am. I'm not sure why this situation is suddenly different."

"Because this summit is critical," Jake said. "Not just when it comes to warfare but when it comes to the potential for another assassination attempt. Things have been quiet since Air Force One six months ago. We need domestic terrorists to see how weak they are and how strong we are. Leaving sends the exact opposite message."

"I get why you feel that way, but how can we just act like this didn't happen? And it's not just the Ambassador. There have been two attempts on the President's life already just since we've gotten here, and it's only the first day. We have several more days of this."

"I don't think that we're going to discourage more attacks by running home and hiding," Jake countered. "In fact, I think we'll encourage more attacks. The right thing to do is to stay and show that we won't be cowed."

Bryan cracked a smile. "You sound like me. Who'da thunk it?"

"To Special Agent Foster's point, sir," Dawson said, "It would be a lot harder to assassinate you in Washington than here."

"Then why have there been three attempts on my life in Washington?"

Dawson's lips thinned a little. "The situation has changed since then. Thanks to Special Agents Mercer and Foster, Washington is now almost impenetrable. Anyone who gets within a half-mile of wherever you are is instantly flagged. Here we don't have that luxury."

"That's another big point," Jess said. "We have resources in Washington that we don't have here. We can have an entire battalion of National Guard respond to the White House within five minutes if we need to."

"Not every assassination attempt is going to be a pitched battle," Jake said. "In fact, most of them won't be. Even Trident has moved away from that and started using subterfuge and trickery to get close. No one's trying to kill the President with a bomb. They're sneaking close with a knife."

"Okay, Jake, but we have more resources to protect against that at home too. We can put Secret Service agents anywhere in Washington. Now, someone could actually get off the damned elevator with an assault rifle, and we'll have to hope that the agents we have can win in a shootout."

"We can win in a shootout," Jake assured her.

"What if the President is on his way out of his room or back to his room when that door opens? What if they take the stairs?"

Jake sighed. "I get everything you're saying, Jess, and believe me, I'm as surprised as you are that I'm advocating that we stay. But we need this. We need the world to see that this peace summit happened. Even if nothing comes out of it right away, we can't have the President lose face. If he does, then the conflicts in Eastern Europe and the Arabian Peninsula grow exponentially worse. Boots on the ground type worse. If we put boots on the ground on one side while Russia puts boots on the ground on the other side, those boots end up marching to each other, and the next thing you know, we're at war with the Russian Federation."

"That's a slippery slope fallacy, Jake."

"It's a slippery slope, but it's not a fallacy."

The President held up a hand. "I've made my decision. The summit will continue as I originally planned. I agree with Jake and stand by my original assertion that we can't show the President of the United States submitting to a terrorist demand. We need to stand firm in the face of this threat, and when—not if, when—it fails, we send a message to every terrorist that we won't be cowed."

"Or we encourage them to make a bigger attack for not listening," Jess said, crossing her arms. "That's another thing terrorists do. They get angry and they throw tantrums. Except they tend to throw tantrums with bombs and guns."

The President met Jess's eyes, and Jess lowered hers. He waited a second, then continued. "I have confidence that all of you will do whatever is necessary to keep me and my family safe. Rest assured, I will follow whatever instructions you give me. I will follow any route you tell me to take, and if I attend the rest of this summit wearing a suit of armed Secret Service agents, so be it. But this summit continues."

"Respectfully, sir," Jess tried one last time, "what do you hope to gain from this summit?"

The President smiled slightly. "I think I know what you're getting at, Jess. You're right. Russia won't have a change of heart here. They might never have a change of heart. No treaties will be signed, no arms reduction agreements and no weapons bans or non-aggression pacts.

"But we will have stood up in the face of adversity and made it clear that we will continue to stand. My opponents like to act like that's an empty gesture, that simply stating that we won't support violence and oppression will have no effect on how the world works. I think they're wrong. People look to us for an example. I intend to set one I would be proud to have my children follow."

Jess finally accepted she was beaten. She lowered her eyes and nodded.

"Wonderful," Bryan said. "I want all of you to get some rest. And don't panic. They've been trying for me for a year and a half now, and I'm still alive and kicking. They clearly haven't done their homework, or they'd no better than to face you guys."

He left for his room, and Dawson took the opportunity to excuse himself and assume his post outside of the President's door.

Jess kept her eyes down and wouldn't meet Jake's gaze. Jake could tell that she was furious with him, but she kept her cool remarkably well. When Jake said, "Can we go to your room to strategize?" she nodded and said, "Of course."

When the door to her room closed behind them, though, she didn't hold back. "What the hell happened, Jake? Since when do you advocate staying somewhere dangerous?"

"Everywhere is dangerous, Jess. We've had traitors in the Secret Service. We've had domestic terrorists and international terrorists all try to kill the President. Everywhere we look, there's danger."

"Look me in the eye and tell me that the United States is as dangerous as Russia."

"I think it might be," Jake said. "Until Bard is brought to justice, there's always at least a sniper's chance."

Jake regretted that instantly. His old friend, Andrew McNeill, *was* a sniper, and a damned good one, nearly as good as Jake himself. He was Bard's right hand man and knowing that he could kill the President from a distance made him possibly the greatest threat the President faced.

Jess knew that too. "Yeah, and your old buddy might actually be that sniper." She sighed. "I still feel like we're stuck in a tent in the middle of a hurricane when we could be in a reinforced bunker or a nuclear bomb shelter."

"I know how you feel," Jake said. "But don't lose hope. It's us we're talking about. Hell, you and I were literally hogtied on board Air Force One facing the two best agents in the Secret Service, and we managed to untie ourselves—no, *you* managed to untie us—and we took the airplane back and got the President down safely. There's nothing they can do to hurt us."

Jess grinned at him. "That makes *us* the best Secret Service Agents."

"Atta girl. Now I know you love proving me wrong, but I need you to help me figure out the President's itinerary and prove me right."

She laughed and said, "Well, if you insist. So, since we're very foolishly agreeing to stay in the lions' den instead of doing the smart thing and taking the obvious right course of action by heading home, the best thing we can do is be completely unpredictable. I'm talking turn-by-turn unpredictable."

"Randomized routes?"

"Randomize in the moment. The drivers on earpieces going where I tell them to go immediately and without question or prior knowledge of any of my decisions, which, in any case, will be made randomly and in the moment."

"That's a good idea."

"Of course it is. It's my idea. Also, I suggest that you stay back here with me."

Jake frowned. "Okay, not sure how I feel about that one."

"Yes, you are. You hate it. But that doesn't make it a bad idea."

Jake's frown deepened. "If I'm not with the President—"

"Then it will be no different then when you went cowboy looking for the guy who made that phone call this morning. You stay with me so you can issue commands as needed and go wherever you need to go at a moment's notice. Just like during the White House attack. You led the troops—no pun intended—and when you had to intervene personally, you were able to do so right away. Frankly, we've enjoyed most of our success when you take a leadership role at ten thousand feet instead of being a boot on the ground."

Jake nodded. "I get it, but... well, but I hate it."

"I hate that we're still here. So deal with it."

Jake shook his head. "Okay. So I'm back here. If that's the case, then I want the RRT following the President."

"Absolutely. It's the least we can do after what happened in China. Russia will throw a fit, but they'll have to get over it. It's clear that American diplomats aren't safe in foreign countries, and the President is *the* diplomat."

"What do we do about the FSB?"

"We feed them information and make sure it's false every time. They keep fucking up and acting on it, thus proving that they're up to no good and losing face."

Jake smiled. "I like the way you think."

"I'm glad to hear it. Aren't you grateful that I'm not incredibly pissed at you for disagreeing with me in there and choosing to take it out on you by lapsing into stony silence?"

"I am. Am I correct to assume that the stony silence will occur the moment this assignment is over?"

"Nah. I'm just going to make you buy me an even fancier dinner than last time."

Jake groaned. "Not lobster again."

"Well, it was going to be steak, but now it's going to definitely include lobster since you hate it so much."

"Why? It's just a big fucking shrimp! Why do people spend so much money on it?"

"I'm sorry to know that your palate is so weak. I happen to think that it's the most delicious seafood on Earth. If you hate it, you can order yourself a bucket o'shrimp from the Gumbo Gallery, but I'm getting my damned lobster with butter sauce."

"What's wrong with the Gumbo Gallery?"

Jess stared at him a moment, then sighed and shook her head. "You're what's wrong with America."

They parted in good spirits, but the moment Jake was out of Jess's room, his smile faded. He stood by his position that they should stay in Moscow, but he shared all of Jess's fears.

They *were* in more danger here. They were cut off from resources. They were cut off from their friends. They were at risk from whoever was trying to assassinate the President.

And Jake had just encouraged the President to stay in—as Jess so aptly put it—the lions' den.

CHAPTER TEN

They left the hotel an hour earlier than normal and fifteen minutes before they announced their departure. It took Jess an extra thirty minutes to lead them through the convolute route to the Kremlin.

Jake spend the entire time sitting next to Jess in her hotel room, his knuckles white on his knees as he waited for one of the agents in the field to announce an attack. When the motorcade arrived safely and Dawson reported that the President was inside the Kremlin, Jake released a heavy sigh of relief.

"Good work agents," he said. "Wonderful. Keep me posted on the situation inside. If anything out of the ordinary happens at all, I want to know—"

His phone rang. He frowned and finished, "Yesterday."

He tapped his earpiece then picked up his phone. Jess frowned questioningly at him, and he shook his head. *I don't know.*

Jake half-expected this to be another anonymous warning. When the voice turned out to be Kaspov instead, he wasn't exactly reassured.

"How did you get this number?"

"Special Agent, please. I'm not a babe in the woods. You've done well randomizing the President's route. I'm impressed. Of course, since my agency is only trying to help ensure his safety, it's extraordinarily frustrating that you don't trust me, but even my poor field agents have admitted that short of trusting us to be at least intelligent enough to know that working with you is smarter than working against you, randomizing the President's movements is the best way to prevent an assassination."

"Why are you calling, Kaspov?"

"Because I have information that you'll want me to share."

"And what is that?"

"A lead on the poison used to attack your President."

"You know who poisoned him?"

"Yes. Did we not establish this? The hotel employee you and I spoke with. She was hired to poison him."

"I know that. I mean, do you know who hired her."

"Ah. No, but she mentioned that the person who hired her obtained the poison from Viper's Alley."

"What's Viper's Alley?"

"It's a neighborhood in downtown Moscow. The real downtown Moscow, not the tourist-slash-government sector. I'll send your partner the coordinates."

Jess flinched and gasped when her laptop announced that it was receiving a download. Jake's eyes narrowed. The information he was getting might very well be helpful, but that wasn't why Kaspov was sending it. He was sending a message. *I can see you even when you don't want me to see you. I can get to you even when you don't want me to get to you.*

Jake suddenly wished he had supported Jess and advocated to return to the states. Not that it would have made a difference. When the President made a decision, he didn't back down from it. He wanted to stay in Moscow so they would stay there no matter what happened.

"Have you received the data?" Kaspov asked, his smug tone indicating that he was aware of the shock he had just given the American agents.

"You have no right to have access to our computers."

"Please stop being naïve, Mercer. We both know the game we're playing. We are allies of convenience, nothing more. You have acted deceitfully to me. I understand why, but surely you can understand why it's important to me to make it clear to you that I will ascertain the truth regardless of your attempts at deception. Now, shall we continue beating our chests, or would you like the information I have for you?"

Jake's grip tightened around his cell phone, but he forced himself to remain calm. "Tell me what you know."

"There is a woman in Viper's Alley known as Baba Yaga. Pardon the stereotypical nickname. We Russians love our traditions. She is notorious in the criminal underworld for selling poisons. It's believed that seventy percent of the assassinations in the Eastern Bloc in the past twenty years have been facilitated by her poisons. I don't know where to find her, so don't ask. I only know she's in Viper's Alley. The best way to get a hold of her, I imagine, would be to make it known that you're in the market. You'll have to sell it well, or they'll make you for an infiltrator, and no one will talk to you. I advise that you say you need it to kill your ex-wife. When you are approached by an intermediary, insist on seeing Baba Yaga. When they refuse, tell them your ex-wife is Anastasia Valuev."

"That's a very specific guess."

"Take it as you will. But I will not send one of my own agents to Viper's Alley. We have a great deal of undercover work going on there, and I don't want to compromise it."

"Who's Anastasia Valuev?"

"You don't need to know that."

"What if they ask me who she is to make sure I'm telling the truth."

A pause. "Well played. Very well. She is the mistress of the Minister of the Interior. He is quite fond of her. If she were at death's door, then someone holding an antidote to that poison could be in a position of great power."

"So I'm asking for an antidote too?"

"No, only the poison. Baba Yaga must covet this power for herself. She will see the opportunity and speak to you in person in order to ensure you aren't lying to her. Then you pounce."

"Pounce?"

Kaspov sighed. "Must you be so dense? You apprehend her, take her somewhere and question her. You can handle a few underworld thugs without being killed, yes?"

Jake thought of the three men he'd beaten earlier. "I can. But if this is you trying to separate me—"

"Then the moment you don't come back, I contend with your very wrathful partner and all the resources she can command. Sometimes people are who they say they are, Special Agent."

"And who are you?"

"An ally."

Jake looked at Jess. She shook her head slightly. *Bad Idea.*

But if Kaspov was telling the truth, then maybe they could trace the assassination back to the assassin. It would be another link in the chain.

"All right. Let's get this done."

"Good. And just to show that I'm not an animal, if you get into trouble, call me, and my officers will rescue you."

Over my dead body. "I will. Thank you."

He hung up, and Jake turned to Jess. She glared at him, and he sighed and said, "I know. But what choice do we have?"

"To do literally anything else."

"I need your help with this, Jess."

She sighed. "Lobster dinner and a very nice pair of earrings."

"I can't buy you jewelry. Sheila will get jealous."

"So buy her two pairs of earrings."

"You're killing me."

"The way you're going, you're killing yourself."

***

An hour later, Jake found himself in a dirty, rundown street market in a part of Moscow that definitely didn't remind Jake of Washington, D.C. but bore a disturbing resemblance to seedier parts of Los Angeles that Jake remembered from his Marine Corps days training at Camp Pendleton in Southern California.

The only sign that it was a market were the not-so-hidden drug and weapons deals taking place in almost flagrant view. There were no stalls and no buskers. Everyone seemed to know who was who.

Which meant that everyone knew immediately who *wasn't* who. Jake attracted attention almost immediately, and it became clear just as quickly that he was American.

"You need to learn some foreign languages," Jess said in his earpiece.

"Let's just get this done as quickly as possible."

"Oy!" a voice called in thickly accented English. "You!"

Jake turned to see a thickset man with more hair on his arms than his head moving his way. He glared at Jake and said, "What are you doing here? This is not for tourists. You need to leave."

"I married a Russian woman," Jake said, "but she was unfaithful. I went to seek my revenge, but the man she is cheating on me with is someone I can't easily get to. So I'm going for her instead."

The man rolled his eyes. "We are not wedding counselors here. Come. I'll escort you out. I won't hurt you, but believe me little man, this is not the place for you."

He grabbed Jake's arm with surprising gentleness but unmistakable firmness. He was probably a bouncer at his day job.

"I am going to kill Anastasia," he said. "She calls herself Valuev now, but her last name is Billings whether she admits it or not. I wish to speak to Baba Yaga."

The big man stopped. He searched Jake's face and said, "You are not Anastasia's husband."

There was no doubt in that statement. *Shit.*

"I wish to speak to Baba—"

"I will take you to her, but you are not here to kill your ex-wife. Why are you here?"

57

Jake hesitated a moment, then decided he was going to be honest. What could it hurt at this point?

"There was an attempt made on someone else's life," he said, "I need to know who bought that poison. I'm not interested in Baba Yaga. She can live forever and kill many more people for all I give a shit. But not the person who was nearly killed the other day."

The man's eyes narrowed. "Come this way."

"Jake," Jess whispered in his earpiece. "What are you doing?"

"Improvising."

"I don't like this."

"Me either."

The big man led Jake to an open door that led into what looked very much like an opium den. People lounged around smoking something thick and sweet-smelling. Jake and his escort stepped over them and headed to another room separated only by a screen.

The man gestured inside with his head. "She's in here. Tell her who you are and what you want. Be honest. There's no need to lie, American. Baba Yaga is smart enough not to make more trouble than she can handle. I hope you are as well."

Jake walked inside and saw a woman in her late twenties sitting cross legged on a pillow in the middle of the room. She was almost completely undressed, wearing only a thin pair of panties and a sheer bra that left almost nothing to the imagination. No doubt that unnerved most people who came to see her, but Jake found the getup a little childish.

The woman smiled at him and said in flawless English. "Special Agent. If I'd known you were coming to visit me, I would have put something more appropriate on. I usually dress like this to intimidate criminals, but I have a feeling it won't have the same effect on you."

"No," Jake agreed. "I need to know who tried to poison the President."

He didn't even bother to ask how she knew he was Secret Service. Clearly, he wasn't as good at keeping things from people as he thought he was.

God, he hated Russia.

She laughed. "I sell people poison every day. I ask them what they use it for because I'm curious, but they don't always tell me the truth. That's how Grigoriy knew you were lying. No one announces in the middle of the street that they're going to kill the mistress of the Minister of the Interior."

Thank you, Kaspov. "Well, congratulations on seeing through my ruse. Truly, you are a wise and strong woman. Now tell me who you sold poison to nine days ago."

"I sold poison to sixteen individuals on that day. It was a slow day."

"So you should remember every one of them."

"I am not superhuman, Special Agent. I only make myself appear that way. There were five women trying to kill abusive husbands—so they said, anyway—three men trying to kill wives, four men trying to kill mothers, and four men trying to kill other men. Those were the stories they told me. No one mentioned anything political, but again, if they were trying to kill the President, that is not information they'd volunteer."

"So you can't tell me anything?"

"Tell her the poison was ricin," Jess suggested.

"What if I told you that the poison was ricin?"

Baba Yaga lifted an eyebrow. "Ah. Well, that would narrow it down to the five women trying to kill husbands. Wait. Four of them. One asked for strychnine."

"Good. Can you give me a description of those women?"

She laughed. "They were all dirty blondes, middle aged, squat and short. I don't remember their eyes, so I would guess they were brown or gray. I would notice if they were blue or green."

So, in other words, they looked like everyone else."

"I already told you that I couldn't help you."

Jake sighed. "Lovely. I love wasting my time."

Baba Yaga smiled coquettishly. "If you can waste fifteen more minutes, I promise you I can make that worth your while."

She reached behind and unclasped her bra. It fell to the floor, and Jake sighed and resisted the urge to rub his temples. He turned and left the room without another word. The criminal's laughter followed him all the way out of the room into Viper's Alley.

CHAPTER ELEVEN

The President made it back to the hotel without incident. Part of Jake wished that whoever was doing this would just make a move already so he could catch them and stop them and stop playing this bullshit game.

But the President made it unmolested. He arrived in good spirits. They had begun negotiations in earnest today, and it looked like they had gone well, at least so far. The President's goals were de-escalation of the conflict in Eastern Europe and a ceasefire agreement in the Middle East. Jake couldn't be sure exactly what had been discussed, but he imagined that the Russian President had indicated a willingness to consider those proposals.

Jake wished he felt as optimistic as the President, but finding himself with nowhere to go after a day spent chasing poison to a dead end, he couldn't stifle his frustration. He'd given the description of Baba Yaga's customer to the police, but they had told him what he already knew. "That describes every woman over forty in Moscow."

"I know," Jake had replied glumly. "Just do your best."

Kaspov had offered his condolences when his lead turned out to be a dead end. "Did you avail yourself of her other talents, at least?" he asked.

"I thought you said you'd never seen her."

"So we are both liars. It seems I am simply better at it than you."

Jake hung up on him.

Now, he and Jess sat in her hotel room discussing what precious little they knew so far.

"So we have a straightforward attempt to infiltrate the hotel and kill the President. We have a poisoning attempt, and we have the Ambassador to China killed. We know that an employee was hired to poison the vodka and whoever hired her got that poison from a criminal in Moscow's skid row."

"A very hot criminal."

"Not in the mood, Jess."

"I know. I was there when you rebuffed her advances, remember?"

"Seriously, not in the mood."

60

"Hey, you deal with disappointment by being a grumpy asshole. I deal with it by being funny and telling jokes."

Jake sighed. "Well, how about we deal with it by figuring out what the hell is going on."

"Hot take," Jess said, "this is a chess game."

"What do you mean?"

"Well, let's look at it. First, someone comes to kill the President announcing that Westernization is poisoning the fatherland."

"I didn't know he was arguing that."

"Kaspov and I talked while you were out on your poison hunt."

Jake glared at her. "Okay. What does that have to do with chess?"

"Well, he's the knight, bravely carrying the torch to protect the fatherland."

"All right. I'll bite. What about the poisoning?"

"Are you familiar with Lucrezia Borgia?"

"Yes, but what does that have to do with this?"

"Well, she was a noblewoman. Like a queen."

"That's a bit of a stretch, Jess."

"Maybe. But since we're spitballing, I'm going with it. Besides, she's not the only one. Queens have poisoned kings and lovers for all of human history. Pharoah's consorts have poisoned pharaoh's, Chinese empresses have poisoned emperors, etc. etc."

"Okay, so that's the queen. The ambassador was what, a pawn?"

"A bishop. He was 'taken.'"

"So the knight moves and is taken. The queen moves, but her gambit fails. Then our bishop is taken. So what's next?"

"Well, we didn't castle. That would have been us retreating to Washington, D.C. to hide in our 'fortress.'"

"I know nothing about chess, Jess."

She giggled. "Chess, Jess." Seeing Jake's expression, she said, "Sorry. Honestly, I don't know much either. But I know that our bad guy loves chess. More specifically, he loves outsmarting people. He loves humiliating their enemies by toying with them, showing them how much weaker and less capable they are before killing them."

"So, who's toying with us? Bard?"

"Maybe. But this doesn't seem like him. He's not the type to go after side characters like the Ambassador."

"He went after Kline before sabotaging Air Force One."

"He hired terrorists who happened to have a grudge against Kline. I doubt he's involved in this plot. I would imagine he's learned his lesson about outsourcing."

"So who?"

Jess sighed."I don't know. I wish we knew chess better."

"Well, you know the basics, and we both know how to protect the President. We both have experience with terrorists, and we have a good friend who understands espionage."

"Mr. Topaz?"

"Yep. I'll see if I can get him on the phone."

The CIA operative answered on the first ring, and Jake put the phone on speaker. "Hey, Mercer. Dare I hope this is good news?"

"It's not. The lead on the poison dried up. Whoever bought it looks like every disgruntled housewife in Russia."

"Lovely. Well, you're on the phone with me, so that means you have at least some idea where to go."

"I do, but before we go there, you should know that Kaspov from the FSB has apparently infiltrated all of our electronics. He has the number to my burner phone, and he was able to get into Jess's laptop."

"Was he now?" Topaz sounded amused rather than alarmed. "Well, I'll just have to deal with that little problem on my way over there."

"You're on your way over here?"

"You can kick him out of our systems?" Jess added.

"I can, but I think I'm just going to mess with him a little and put an overlay on your system that will broadcast white noise to him. Or maybe I'll have even more fun and put some cartoon theme songs on a loop."

"Should I be relieved or disturbed that you aren't freaked out by this?"

"Yes. I'll see you two in a few minutes."

He clicked off the line, and Jess and Jake met each other's eyes.

"Christ, I hate spies," Jake said.

Jess offered a nervous laugh. "At least we have better ones."

"Let's hope so."

Topaz arrived ten minutes later, a briefcase in his hand and a sly grin on his face. "Let me guess," Jess said, "You went with the cartoons."

"I did. I expect he will be very annoyed. But let's talk business. You guys want my help finding out who's after the President."

"Yes. We've come to the conclusion that our assassin is playing a chess match with us."

"Do you mean that literally or figuratively?"

"We're not sure," Jake replied. "And it's not really a conclusion yet. More like an impression."

The two Secret Service agents outlined their hypothesis. Topaz listened quietly, his chin resting in his right hand while his left moved in an infinity symbol on the table. The odd mannerism fit with the spook, whose bright gray eyes stared unblinkingly at the two of them as they spoke. When they finished, he said, "Hmm. It's an intriguing theory."

"Do you think it's an accurate one?" Jess asked.

"Good enough for rock and roll," he replied. "Do you have a chessboard?"

"No."

"You came to Russia without a chessboard? For shame. That's all right. I have one."

He lifted his briefcase onto the table and opened it to reveal a carefully organized chess set with ornately carved ivory and ebony pieces and a raised wooden board.

Jake looked at Topaz. "You just randomly brought a chessboard here?"

The spy grinned. "I guessed."

"You must be popular at parties."

"Actually now. People tend to be afraid of me. No idea why."

He set up the board and said, "All right. So this is day zero. Let's go through all of our moves. First"—he moved one of the pawns two spaces forward—"he sends someone to buy poison and hires a hotel employee to place it in the President's vodka. Then"—he moved a knight—"he convinces or pays an ultranationalist nut to try to assassinate the President. We change the President's itinerary." He moved one of the black pawns two spaces ahead. "The knight moves again, and then we take that knight."

He moved the black queen to take the knight. "We're going to be ignoring chess strategy for the purposes of this demonstration," he said, "Obviously, no one would ever open an actual chess game like this, but much as I like games, this is real life, and the moves are different. Anyway, the President's chef opens the bottle of vodka and prepares to cook with it. He thinks, hey, why not take a shot before making dinner?"

Topaz moved another white pawn two spaces forward. "Except our chef isn't a moron, so he sniffs the vodka, thinks, 'huh, that's not right,' and realizes that the liquor is poisoned. Bye bye, poison." He took the pawn with the black pawn.

He leaned back and stared at the board a moment. "We missed a part here," he said. "You get an anonymous tip that leads you to change the President's itinerary in the first place." He moved one of the black pawns ahead. "Our guy kills the person who tipped you." He moved the white bishop to take that pawn. "Ignore the fact that I crossed the queen to do that," he said. "This happened before we moved the queen. Not that it matters because this isn't actually chess."

He took the white bishop with the black bishop. "So that's the ambassador's murder. Now we have a white bishop right next to our king, which freaks us out, but essentially changes nothing because an assassin in Beijing can't do anything to a President in Moscow without making a few more moves. That's represented here by the fact that the bishop can only move diagonally and isn't a threat to any of our pieces at the moment."

"Anyway, we change the President's itinerary again"—he moved another pawn two spaces forward—"and we try to find the source of the poison, but we fail." He took that pawn with the black bishop. "And that's where we are right now."

"So what's his next move?" Jake asked.

"Well, if this were a chess game, his next move would be to resign, apologize for wasting everyone's time and take up checkers. Since this is real life, I would say his next move needs to be to get real intelligence on the President's movements and stop trying to bludgeon his way to the President."

"Kaspov has access to his movements."

"I don't think Kaspov is involved in this," Topaz said. "He's an arrogant, insecure prick, but he's too smart to risk putting his nation at war with us."

"My thoughts exactly," Jess said, beaming at Topaz.

Jake rolled his eyes.

"So our guy needs to get intelligence. Or he needs to act on the intelligence he has. He knows the President will be here at night and at the Kremlin during the day. Those are his two best bets without foreknowledge of a timeline or a route. So he can come after the President here—next to impossible with you guys here—or he can go after The President at the Kremlin—next to impossible because the

64

Russian President is there, and he won't tolerate anything untoward happening without his consent since he's another arrogant, insecure prick."

"So we don't know what his next move is," Jake summarized.

"We know he needs intelligence. Or he needs to clear away all of the pieces currently defending the President so he can get to him."

"How's he going to clear those pieces?"

"I hate to say it," Topaz said, "but it's his move right now. We won't know what our move is until he makes his."

Jake frowned. "I really don't like that."

"Neither do I, but there's nothing we can do about it right now. We'll just have to do our best to keep the President under guard and try to get intelligence of our own. You handle the former, I'll work on the latter."

Jake sighed. "Another day in the life."

"Amen, brother."

CHAPTER TWELVE

For the second time during this summit, Jake was woken by a phone call. Once more, he was awake instantly. He answered his phone as he got to his feet and dressed quickly. "Mercer. Who is this?"

"Jake, it's Jess. There's been a break-in."

Jake's blood froze. "What?"

"There's been a break-in. Someone broke into the President's room and kidnapped Sheila."

The world spun around Jake. He staggered backwards, and only his years of discipline and training allowed him to keep his feet.

"Jake? Are you there?"

Jake took a deep breath and forced himself to be professional. "I'm here. Where is the President?"

"He's in my room right now, along with Special Agent Dawson and his detail. He's... well, Dawson's been forced to hold him back. He's trying to get into his own room, but we need to wait for the gas to dissipate."

In the background, Jake could hear the President shouting, "Is that Jake? Tell him to call off his dogs and let me see my family!"

Jake's heart seemed to pound in his throat rather than his chest. His ears hummed, and his mouth was suddenly dry. "What happened? The room was gassed?"

"Yes. We don't know more than that at the moment. Two of Dawson's agents entered the room but felt faint almost immediately. I called the hotel, and they're cycling the air in that room. We should be able to enter in ten minutes."

"How do you know Sheila's gone?"

"Dawson's agents confirmed that the four agents inside the suite are unconscious, along with the President and the First Lady. Sheila's missing."

"Where was the President?"

"He stepped downstairs for a drink. He was having trouble sleeping."

"Jake!" the President called.

66

Jake heard Bryan grunt, presumably as he struggled with the agents. "Sir!" Dawson called. "Let us handle it!"

"Then fucking handle it!"

"I'm on my way to the President's suite," Jake said. "Do *not* let the President out of that room under any circumstances, and do *not* let anyone in until you see me. Do you understand?"

"Yes."

"Good. Stay on the line in case I pass out."

"Wait, Jake—"

"I can't wait, Jess."

If Jake was able to think clearly, he would have felt guilty for forcing the President to remain outside of the room when he wasn't willing to wait to look for Sheila either, but he was barely able to think at all.

Shiela. Oh God, Sheila. Please no.

He reached the room and walked inside. He breathed deeply and forced the breath out in hard grunts, a technique learned from the Marine Corps to survive low-oxygen environments.

The two agents guarding the door were sprawled just inside the entrance, their weapons a few inches from their outstretched hands. They had evidently entered the room as soon as they heard a commotion and were almost instantly knocked out by the gas.

Jake felt his own head start to pound. The gas was probably much weaker than it had been earlier, considering how quickly it had incapacitated his agents, but Jake needed to move faster. He drew his weapon and proceeded into the room.

Trumbull lay unconscious in the hallway, a cleaver in his hand. Apparently, he had tried to intervene as well.

The door to the President's bedroom lay ajar. A Secret Service agent lay sprawled across the First Lady's body in a bid to protect her. Both she and the First Lady were out cold. A second Secret Service Agent lay on the floor at the foot of the bed in a pool of blood. As far as Jake could tell, he was the only fatality.

And Sheila was gone.

Jake felt his knees go weak, but not from the gas. Once more, he had to call on every ounce of his training to steady himself.

"Jake? Are you there?"

"I'm here. It's true. Sheila's gone."

"Oh God."

***

The President sat ramrod straight at the head of the table. Dawson and his team stood around him, their faces grim and taut with anger. The First Lady sat slumped over to the President's right, breathing heavily, eyes lolling as she slowly regained consciousness. Her bodyguard shook visibly, and his face shone with sweat, but otherwise, he maintained his posture as he stood behind her. The other two agents sat in chairs on either side of the conference room door. They would be nearly useless as guards until they recovered, but hotel security was at every elevator and stairwell, and Moscow Police swarmed the lobby and parking lot.

Jess sat to the President's left, Jake on her own left, her face tense with worry. Her laptop was opened and turned so that the three of them could see the security feed sent upstairs from the camera room.

"So this is our timeline of events," she said, keeping an admirable display of calm. "Two-thirty-five, Cooper and Sarkinian open the front door and rush into the room. They almost immediately start gagging and coughing, then collapse. We don't have footage inside the room, but we can assume that the noise they heard was the kidnapper entering the room and taking Sheila. It looks like he jumped the gun a little because the agents and the chef inside the room were still conscious, albeit briefly. Two-thirty-six..."

A figure dressed in all black and wearing a ski mask walked out of the room, carrying Sheila. The First Lady began to cry softly, still too weak to launch into the hysterics that were sure to come as soon as she regained her strength.

The President sat stock still, stone-faced as he watched the figure reach the maintenance elevator at the far end of the hall.

"Poole and Goering called me at two-thirty-six, around the time the kidnapper entered the elevator. While on the phone with me, Poole called hotel security, who sent a team to intercept the kidnapper. Two-thirty-eight"—she pressed a button on the laptop—"The kidnapper exits the elevator and places Sheila into the back of a UAZ off-road van. He gets into the driver's seat and starts to drive away. Hotel security arrives along with our Counter Assault Team and attempts to barricade the exit. They shoot at the van, but it's got bulletproof glass and armor. They shoot the tires, but they're some sort of military run-flat. Bottom line, is he gets away."

68

"Why?" Carrie whispered. "Why do we always have to come with you, Bryan? Why can't we stay home? This is *your* life, not ours."

Jess lowered her eyes briefly, then lifted them back to her screen. "Two-forty-one. Moscow Police are notified and given the van's description, along with a description for Sheila and as close as we can get for the kidnapper. The President arrives upstairs, and upon seeing the situation, Dawson and his team secure him into my room. The President…" She hesitated, then decided not to mention the President's resistance.

"Two-forty-three. I call Jake, er, Special Agent Mercer, and he confirms that Sheila has been kidnapped, and that all present in the suite are unconscious but alive, with the exception of Special Agent Barnes, who was stabbed to death, presumably in the act of defending the First Daughter."

Carrie lifted her head and stared at Bryan with hate. "You asshole. You fucking asshole. *You* wanted this. We never wanted this. We just wanted *you*. But *you* had to fucking go out for President because you had to be the savior of the world, the leader of the free and the brave. You had to build a legacy so you could get your own fucking face on a goddamned statue in the Smithsonian. How much is enough, Bryan? You know, one of these times, they're going to succeed, right? They're going to kill Sheila and maybe me. They're going to kill us, and it's going to be your fucking fault, you *fucking asshole!"*

She leaped to her feet and swiped at the President viciously. Her nails dug grooves in his cheeks and blood welled in the wounds.

Her bodyguard, Special Agent Fisher, grabbed her and dragged her away. She kicked and shrieked as he led her to the opposite end of the table. When he placed her in another chair, she slumped down and sobbed bitterly.

The President sat stock still, staring straight ahead. Blood trickled down his cheek, but he gave no reaction. Jake could understand. He felt just as numb as Bryan did.

Jess looked at Jake to see if she should continue. Jake took a breath and forced himself to be present. "For the time being, the President will remain in this room. When Chef Trumbull is cleared medically, he will return to the suite in the company of Special Agent Poole. If the First Lady desires, she can remain here, or she can return to the suite. The Presidential Security Detail will remain here at the President's side."

Bryan stirred for the first time. "I have to go to the summit, Jake. I can't stop now. Too many civilians are dying."

"Oh yeah, go to your summit," Carrie called from the other side of the table. "Go ahead. That's what's important, right?"

Bryan met Carrie's eyes. "I'm sor—"

"Don't you fucking *dare* say that to me!"

Jake had to agree with Carrie. He understood the importance of ending the wars in Ukraine and Syria as soon as possible, but this was one situation where the President would be entirely justified in calling negotiations to a halt.

But if Bryan was so set on continuing these negotiations with his daughter missing, then there was nothing Jake or anyone else could do to persuade him otherwise.

"All right," Jake said. "Dawson, you and your men shadow the President at all times wherever he goes. Coordinate with the FSB to ensure his safety along the route to the Kremlin."

"Should we continue to randomize the route, sir?"

"Yes. You're in charge of that. Special Agent Foster and I will work with Moscow Police to find Sheila."

"Or her body," the First Lady interrupted. "Because you know that's probably what they'll find, right, Bryan?"

Jake stood. He couldn't listen to this anymore. "Jess. With me."

"That's right," Carrie called after him. "Go get her, knight in shining armor. She chooses men just like her mother."

Jake and Jess remained silent as they headed back to her room. As soon as the door closed, Jess said, "Jake, I'm so sorry—"

"Not now, Jess. Just… please."

Jess lowered her eyes and nodded.

"I'm going after him," Jake said. "I want all the info you can get on that van. We'll start there."

His phone rang, and when Jake saw the private number, he expected Kaspov to be on the other end. He forced his irritation aside. The FSB agent might have information for him.

"Mercer."

"Ah, Mercer. So that is your name."

The voice, like Kaspov's, was Russian and cultured and spoke very good English. Unlike Kaspov's baritone, this voice was a soft tenor.

Jake frowned. "Who is this? How did you get this number?"

"It is my business to know things. As far as who I am, my name is Nikolai Ivanovich. Your friend Kaspov will know me. But that is not what you want to talk about right now."

"What do I want to talk about right now?"

"Jake!"

Jake turned to Jess, who had her laptop open and was staring in horror at the screen. Jake walked to her, and when he saw what she did, he gasped and stiffened.

Sheila was bound to a chair and gagged with a rubber ball attached to her by a leather strap. She stared fearfully at the camera, tears streaming down her cheeks, her shoulders shaking with sobs.

Nikolai's gloating voice came over the phone. "That is what you want to talk about."

CHAPTER THIRTEEN

"You have fucked up in the worst way possible," Jake said. "Did you not see what happened the last two times someone threatened the President's daughter? What do you think will happen to you when I find you?"

"What happens to me isn't important," Nikolai replied. "Like you, I am a servant of my country. I want only to give Russia the future it is due."

"And you think provoking a war with the United States is the way to do that?"

"This will not provoke a war. Your President's legacy depends on peace. He has fought his entire tenure for a cessation to conflict. If he reverses course now, history will describe him as weak and spineless."

"Do you really think he'll care about that with his daughter's life on the line?"

"Of course he will. Even if you don't believe, as I do, that all politicians value their legacy above all else, think what the consequences of belligerence will be. Should he sentence thousands of sons, daughters, husbands and wives, mothers and fathers to death for his one daughter?"

"He should show that the enemies of our nation can't act with impunity against us. He will show that."

Nikolai sighed. "It is pointless to argue with you about this. For the sake of our conversation, let's just say that I'm willing to risk war to gain what I want. It is not accurate, but if it allows you to move forward."

Nikolai's condescending smugness galled Jake. His fists clenched, and he gripped his phone so tightly he thought he might crack the case. He took a breath and said, "The bottom line is that the President's daughter needs to be returned to us unharmed, or you will suffer greatly."

"I have suffered greatly. I still suffer. I see the laughingstock the fatherland has become, and I weep."

"Tough shit. That's what you get when you try to bully the rest of the world."

"How ironic to hear that from an American. But we are sidetracked again. I will return the First Daughter to you unharmed, but you must do something for me."

"That's not how this works, Nikolai. You need to give her back now. Period. There are no deals. She comes back, or you die. If you're lucky."

"This will go much faster and more easily if you stop threatening me. I truly don't care what happens to me. So, shall I kill her in front of you, or shall I return her?"

"Don't fuck with me."

Nikolai sighed. He spoke in Russian, and a moment later, a masked figure stepped behind Sheila. He grabbed a fistful of her hair and yanked her head back. She cried out, and the masked figure pressed a combat knife to her throat.

"Wait!" Jake cried.

Nikolai shouted a command, and the masked figure stopped.

Jake shook with fury, but it was impotent fury. There was nothing he could do. "What do you want?" he asked softly.

"I want the President."

Jake's eyes narrowed. "Are you working with Trident?"

"No, Special Agent. I don't blame you for believing that. After all, they've been a thorn in your side for quite some time. But no. I owe them a debt for showing me the vulnerabilities in your system that allowed me to arrive where I am now, but I am acting for Russia. Trident acts for your own nation."

"If you want the President, then why take his daughter?"

"Luck. Poor luck, in this case. I tried to poison him, but his chef has a truly world class palate that I didn't anticipate. I attempted to have a dissident assassinate him, but you cleverly changed the route, and my friend was left stranded. I intended to have the President killed this morning, but he was not in his suite. His insomnia has saved his life and thrown a rather sizable wrench into my plans. You should thank your God, if you worship one.

"So, my checkmate will have to wait. I *do* have you in check now, though. Your choices are to surrender the President, or I will kill the First Daughter. It will be highly inconvenient for me to kill her, because it leaves me at square one with your President, but it will be far more inconvenient for me to allow you to influence the course of events."

"You're insane."

"So what?"

Jake gritted his teeth and forced himself to maintain the appearance of calm. "I can't 'give' you the President. He's under guard, and those guards will remain at his side regardless of what I say. The moment I do anything out of the ordinary, I'll be stopped by his security forces. The short version of what I just said is that I can do everything in my power to give you the President, and all that will happen is I die."

"Agent please. Think outside the box. I realize that is not your agency's specialty, but you must have at least some intelligence to bring to bear to this conundrum. You obviously cannot bind the President and hand him to me in a gift-wrapped sack. But you *can* arrange to leave him vulnerable. You can leave a hole in his protection that will allow me to attack. You can even do it in a way that leaves you appearing innocent. Just think for a moment."

"You're insane."

"No. I'm well-informed. I know that you love her. I know you won't let anything happen to her. So I know that you'll think of a way to give me what I want so that you aren't forced to watch me have her killed."

Jake thought a moment. He obviously couldn't give Nikolai access to the President, but he couldn't deny him outright, or he would watch that knife slice Sheila's throat open. The only thing he could do right now was barter for time.

"Listen... I..." he sighed. "Look, I can't just say yes and then tell you the plan."

"So say yes, and tell me the plan later."

That was promising. "How will I contact you?"

"I will contact you."

"But I need time to figure out how to do this."

"That shouldn't be difficult since it is the only thing with which you will occupy your mind until I contact you. I will not agree to *your* terms, Agent. These are mine. I accept that you lack the intelligence to come up with a plan in this instance. So I will give you time. How much will be up to me. When I call you back, you will tell me how you plan to deliver the President into my hands, and if I like it, I will release Sheila. If I don't, I will slaughter her and find another way to get to your President. Do not waste time, Agent. I am only patient when it suits me."

The video feed cut off, Jake's phone went silent. He set it calmly down on the table and took deep breaths to calm himself. Jess watched

74

him, her eyes wide with fear. He wasn't entirely sure if she was afraid of Nikolai or of himself.

Finally, he spoke. "Contact Mr. Topaz. Bring him up to speed with everything that's happened and tell him we need to find Sheila ASAP. We need to find Nikolai too. It's a good bet that he's not in the same place as Sheila. Once you've done that, contact Moscow Police like we talked about before. I'm going to look for her."

"What about the President?"

"We can't give him up, Jess."

"I know that, but what do we tell Nikolai when he calls back?"

"We'll get to that. Right now, we need to get the actual actions we're going to take in motion. Then we come up with a cover story. He'll give us some time. He knows that it's going to be difficult to make this happen."

Jess nodded. "Are you going to be okay?"

"This is the wrong time to ask me that."

"It isn't, though," she said gently. "I need to know if you think you're too compromised to handle the President's security. If so, then maybe you can turn command to Dawson and focus on retrieving Sheila."

Jake nodded. "You're right to ask that question. That's exactly what I'm doing. Dawson will handle the President's security, and I will handle the rescue. You will provide logistical support for both of us."

"Okay." She reached forward and squeezed his arm. "She'll be okay, Jake. You've done this before. They keep trying, and they keep failing. This is no different."

Jake managed another nod, but Jess was wrong. This *was* different. This was utterly and completely different. The first time Sheila's life was in danger, Jake knew exactly where she was. He was able to get to her within minutes. The second time, Jake's own life was in danger, and their kidnappers didn't want to kill them but only to hold them until they could blackmail Trident.

This time, Jake had no doubt that Nikolai would do exactly as he intended to do. If Jake didn't give up the President, then Sheila would die. Jake didn't know where she was, he didn't know anything about Nikolai, his background or his capabilities. He could make some assumptions, but—

Your friend Kaspov will know me.

Jake sighed. He didn't relish the thought of asking Kaspov for help after the conflict between the two of them. He knew that the Russian

Agent would more likely than not want something in return for his help, probably something that Jake didn't have the authority to give.

But Jake had no choice. Sheila was in danger.

He picked up his phone and dialed the number.

CHAPTER FOURTEEN

"Oh, is this Special Agent Mercer? Not his secretary with the CIA? I am surprised. I thought we were no longer on speaking terms."

"Can it, Kaspov. I need your help."

"You must really need my help if you're calling me. Can your friends with the CIA not use their vast knowledge of Russia to help you?"

Jake suppressed an urge to reach through the phone and strangle Kaspov. "The President's daughter has been kidnapped. There was an attempt on his life this morning. The President happened to be downstairs getting a drink, or he'd be dead right now. Since he wasn't there, the killer took his daughter instead."

Kaspov sighed, and the sarcasm disappeared behind true irritation. "This is why I wanted you and I to work together, Special Agent. You are not in your country; you are in mine. Had you not cut me off from the beginning out of superstitious fear that I would try to assassinate him myself, I would have had resources present to address this situation before it got out of hand."

"Yes," Jake agreed. "I made a mistake. I will point out, though, that you entered this arrangement intent on demonstrating how much smarter and more capable you were than us. You hacked into my partner's computer and stole my private phone number. I made a choice to protect the President because you acted disingenuously. In hindsight, that was the wrong choice, but put yourself in my shoes. If the CIA did the same thing to your President, how would you react?"

Kaspov was silent for a moment. Then he said, a little grudgingly. "Fair enough. I am used to playing a different game than you. My reaction would have been entirely appropriate were you CIA, and for the record, any member of a Russian agency would have done the same. I suppose the differences between American agencies are more sharply defined than those between Russian agencies. I can commit to transparency going forward if you can commit to the same."

"I can."

"All right, then. Do you have any information on the kidnappers? Anything at all? Age, gender, vehicles, weapons? Even the smallest detail could be important."

"I have a name."

"You have a *name?*"

"Yes. He called me a few minutes ago."

"Who called you?"

"Nikolai Ivanovich."

Kaspov remained silent for so long that Jake thought he had hung up. "Kaspov?"

"I'm here."

Kaspov's voice was toneless. Nikolai was right. Kaspov knew him.

"Who is he?" Jake asked.

"He is former KGB, like me. He was renowned in the agency for his brilliance and manipulative ability. He could anticipate the moves of his opponents before they knew those moves themselves, and he could create circumstances that forced those moves to work for Russia's benefit. I won't share the operations he was involved in, but I will say that if you think of a Soviet success in the latter half of the 1980s, Nikolai probably had a hand in them."

"What does he do now?"

"He has a security consultant firm, but I don't know how involved he is with it. He took the dismantling of the Communist Party hard. He believes that Russia was humiliated, and he yearns for a return to Russian supremacy."

"And you don't?"

"Enough with the insults, Special Agent. We're on the same side. Of course, I am a patriot. I will shed no tears if the United States collapses and we emerge supreme. But I am also not a fool. If we attempt to force that change now, the United States will flatten us. Your military is absurdly powerful compared to all other nations on Earth. You have had dubious success when it comes to land engagements, but it won't matter whether you conquer us if you bomb us into glass. I do not desire a war with your nation. I like your military leaders spineless and hesitant, the way they have been for the past thirty years."

"Good one," Jake said drily. "But Nikolai is different?"

"Nikolai wishes to topple the United States. He is not content to wait for you to rot from the inside like all empires. He wants to bring that end about now. He has lost many friends in government because he has advocated for actions that our current leaders do not support. He sees *them* as spineless puppets of the Western regime and is taking matters into his own hands."

"Okay, so we have motive," Jake said. "And if he runs his own private security firm, that explains the resources. So how do we find him?"

"That is like looking for a needle in a stack of identical needles placed in the middle of a field of similar stacks. This is Russia, Special Agent. We are nearly twice the size of your own country."

"He sent me a video of the President's daughter bound in a room somewhere. This was an hour and a half after he kidnapped her."

"Ah. Now we're getting somewhere. That means she is close. What other details can you provide me?"

"He was with someone else. A large, muscular man who wore a mask and carried a combat knife."

"You have described a third of Russian men under the age of sixty, but that's all right. What about the room?"

Jake shook his head. "Concrete walls, concrete floor. No windows that I could see. Hallways on either side of the rear of the room, or at least whatever part of the room was behind Sheila."

"That sounds like a military bunker of some sort. Did you see any sign of radio or computer equipment?"

"No, the only furniture in the room was the chair that Shiela sat on."

"And just to make sure, Shiela is the President's daughter?"

"Yes. That's her name."

"I see. What you have described is probably a standard bomb shelter. No frills, so not a barracks and no equipment, so not a command bunker."

"He issued commands to the man with a knife, though," Jake said. "I doubt he's in the same bunker she is."

"I doubt that as well. Most likely, the armed man had a phone of his own. You said you had the vehicle. What was it?"

Jake looked at Jess. Jess cleared her throat and said, "It was a UAZ van. Armored with military tires."

"That supports the conclusion that she is being held in a military bunker somewhere. If the van is armored, then it is not standard issue. Probably one that his firm modified."

"Does his firm have armored bunkers?"

"They're not supposed to, but if he's bribed the right officials, then they could have bunkers. Or hell, no one checks anything anymore. He could parade down Moscow with a sign that says, 'In ten minutes, I will destroy the Kremlin,' and no one will look twice."

Jake hadn't heard anxiety from Kaspov before. It did little to ease his fears. "If this guy is so dangerous, why has he been allowed to walk free all these years?"

"Because he's kept his hands clean. He's barely involved in his own firm, that we know of, at least. He potters around playing chess with people at bars and reminiscing about the good old days. Most Russians his age reminisce about the Soviet Union. Despite what your media would have you believe, Russian citizens were not overjoyed when the nation broke up. We tolerate people who lament the old glory days. What we don't tolerate is people who act on it. Nikolai will become a pariah *now*, but if he's gone this far, it's likely that he doesn't care about that."

"He said as much."

"What else did he say? Why did he call you? To bribe you with her life?"

"Yes. He wanted me to give him the President in exchange for her."

"Is he a fool? There's no way you'd agree to that."

"He thought that since she and I were… since we…"

Kaspov sighed. "Oh God. You're sleeping with her."

"We're in love," Jake said.

His face flamed as he realized how foolish he sounded, but dammit, it was true. So what if it was against the rules? He couldn't help how he felt.

"Of course you are," Kaspov said drily. "So what did you tell him?"

"That I'd think of a way to give him the President."

"And how do you intend to do that?"

"I don't."

"Obviously not," Kaspov snapped. "What *lie* do you intend to tell him?"

"I'm not sure. I was hoping we could find him and rescue Sheila before it has to go that far."

Kaspov sighed. "*Bozhe moy.* You really need to learn how to behave with intelligence agents. How much time do you have?"

"I don't know. He said he'd tell me."

Kaspov fell silent again for a moment, then said incredulously, "You can't be serious."

"I was afraid for her life. He said he'd kill her if—"

"He's not going to kill his only leverage after a five-minute conversation, Special Agent! You should have insisted on twenty-four hours at least for a plan. *Blin...* Okay, this is what you'll tell him. You'll tell him that you will stage an attack on the President's motorcade. When that attack happens, you will escort the President from the motorcade and take him down a 'hidden route' to safety. You will communicate this hidden route to him, and you will turn the President over to his agents. *Demand* to see Sheila before you turn him over."

"I can't separate the President from the—"

"For God's sake! You will *lie* to him. *Lie*, Special Agent. To be as clear as I can possibly make it, this is what you will *tell* Nikolai, not what you will actually do. When you tell him this, you will tell him that you will have to get him the details the day of the plan. That will buy you an extra day before he will decide you are lying to him."

"What if he doesn't believe me?"

"Then Sheila will die. That is the risk your President has taken bringing his family here. There are no guarantees of success, Special Agent. If there were, the United States would be swearing allegiance to the People's Party.

"Keep me posted on everything that happens. The FSB will do everything in its power to find Sheila, so answer my call when it comes, because when it comes, I will have information for you. And for the love of God, Special Agent, speak from a place of authority when you talk to Nikolai. You are not in check right now. He is. That's why he's behaving desperately."

"I'll do my best."

"That's not good enough," Kaspov snapped. "The fate of both of our nations is in your hands."

He hung up without waiting for Jake to respond. Jake lowered his phone, took a deep breath, and let it out slowly.

"Did you get all that?" Jess said.

"I got it," Topaz's voice said over her laptop's speakers. "I hate to pile it on, Jake, but he's right. You handled the situation with Nikolai poorly."

"Well, that's very goddamned helpful, Topaz," Jake snapped. "What do you suggest I do now, considering that I can't go back in time?"

"I suggest you do exactly what Kaspov said to do. Let us look for the President's daughter. You focus on protecting the President. I promise you, we'll keep you abreast of everything, and if there's anything you can do that will help, we'll let you do it. But you need to think of this as a medical emergency. You're not a doctor, and you can't fix a brain bleed, no matter how much it hurts to see the woman you love injured. Kaspov and I are the doctors. We might work for rival hospitals, but with a person's life on the line—in this case, two nations and probably the world—we'll set those differences aside and work together. You wait for our call and remember: Nikolai wants the President. Protecting him *is* your priority."

Jake had never felt so helpless in his life. Not even when he was bound hand and foot on Air Force One. He had both arms and both legs now. He just couldn't use them.

He lowered his gaze, grateful that only Jess could see him right now. "All right."

"Good."

Jess's laptop beeped softly to indicate the connection was dead. The two Secret Service agents sat in silence for a long moment.

Finally, Jess broke that silence. "What do you want to do?"

Jake took a deep breath and released it in a heavy sigh. "It doesn't matter what I want to do. We're not in control of this situation anymore. We'll do what Topaz and Kaspov recommend."

Jess lowered her eyes. She lifted a hand to Jake but let it fall before it reached him.

Jake tried to put his mind to the task of protecting the President, but all he could think about was the look of terror in Sheila's eyes as her kidnapper held a knife to her throat.

I'm sorry, Sheila. I'm so sorry.

Even unspoken, the words sounded hollow.

CHAPTER FIFTEEN

Jake expected the phone call from Nikolai to come at any moment. As he rode in the command vehicle with Jess, he checked his phone almost constantly, waiting for Nikolai to call and demand an answer.

Jess did a better job than he did of maintaining her cool. She kept in contact with Dawson in the President's vehicle just ahead. All of them were on edge. The seemingly effortless infiltration of their defenses by an enemy operative had left them shaken.

The First Lady had to be sedated before they left. After Jake and Jess had left the conference room, she had flown into another rage and attacked the President again. Dawson didn't share all of the details out of respect for the First Lady and the President, but he did tell Jake that she was moved to another room on the same floor and given sleeping pills to help her rest.

The public, of course, was outraged. There were calls to go to war with Russia, calls to assassinate the Russian president and even calls to kidnap his family and hold them hostage until Sheila was returned.

Through all of this, the President had managed to bury his feelings under a veneer of professionalism. Jake wasn't sure whether to admire him for it or hate him for it.

He wasn't sure whether to admire or hate himself for his inability to focus. Strictly speaking, he had dealt with the compromise well by delegating to Dawson and Jess and effectively removing himself from the decision-making process. That being said, it had been proven once and for all that an attempt on Sheila *would* impact his ability to perform his job.

"Five minutes to the Kremlin, Dawson," Jess said. "We can just head straight there, now. We'll have hundreds of officers here in seconds if anyone tries anything."

"Roger that."

Jake's mind wandered to a conversation he and Sheila had a year ago or so when the President and his family visited Paris only to end up trapped by an outbreak of an engineered super virus. Jake and Sheila were hiding in a CIA safehouse in a forest outside of Paris, and Sheila confided in Jake that she hoped one day to leave politics and

Washington itself behind completely and spend the rest of her life living a simple existence in a rural area close to nature. She clearly hoped for Jake to want the same thing, but at the time, he wasn't sure that he did.

Now? Well, now he wondered. Despite the pressure and risk of his job, he enjoyed being a Secret Service Agent. Even combatting Trident and their various terrorist cohorts, he enjoyed the risk, the danger, and most of all, the chance to overcome great odds and show the enemies of the United States that nothing they could do would stop him.

But it had worn on him. He had suffered severe illness and severe injury. He had suffered more anxiety in the past eighteen months than he had in his entire career in the Marine Corps. He had nearly lost the President more times than he could count, and he had nearly lost Sheila three times. This third time, he might actually lose her.

He didn't know if he could do it anymore. He would rescue Sheila now, no matter what. He would get her and the President home safely, but after that? Would he really stay in this job for the rest of his life? Could he continue to risk losing everything he loved?

Three more years. Three more years, and Bryan would have finished his second term and by law be out of office. Sheila would no longer be obligated to be the supportive daughter, and she and Jake could retire and live somewhere simply and quietly. He had always thought that he could never sit still, but if the other option was to continue to miss out on a chance at a family and a future, could he honestly put the job first?

Few Secret Service agents had lasting relationships. The reason for it was clear. Families got in the way of duty. Many agents were divorced, choosing to put their jobs ahead of their families. Those agents that had families inevitably left or washed out of the service because they couldn't dedicate themselves to their families and still keep their jobs.

Jake knew when he started dating Sheila that he would inevitably have to make a choice between her and his career. He knew now that he had already made his choice. It wasn't right for Jess and Dawson to have to pick up his slack because the woman he loved was in danger. This job didn't come with the same rights other jobs did. There was never an excuse to be anything other than one hundred percent. But he was less than one hundred percent now, and nothing he could do would change that.

So it was time to leave. Not now. Not while Sheila's father was still in office, but as soon as he was out, Jake was out.

"Jake?"

Jake looked up to see they had arrived. Jess was looking at him with concern. "Right." He opened his door and got out. "I'm going to meet with Kaspov. I'll be back in time for the President's departure, but in the meantime, I'm going to look for leads."

"Good luck, Jake. I'll be here in the car with my laptop open and my headset on. I can't add any value to Dawson's team right now besides monitoring, so I'll be able to help you too."

He managed a smile he didn't feel. "Thank you, Jess."

He left the car, and almost immediately, Kaspov found him. "I have someone for you to talk to, Special Agent. He is an old comrade of Nikolai's. They fell out shortly after the KGB was disbanded. He holds no love for Nikolai and has agreed to tell us what he knows of him that could aid in our investigation."

"If he hasn't been close with Nikolai in decades, what can he tell us that's useful?"

"We'll find out."

Jake frowned, but he didn't have a better idea. He followed Kaspov to a waiting car. Jake hesitated briefly before entering, but he would have to take this risk. If Kaspov turned out to be a traitor, it wouldn't be the first time Jake had to extricate himself from that situation.

The car pulled away from the Kremlin and headed toward a seedier part of the city. Jake recognized it after a moment. "We're going to Viper's Alley?"

"Nearby. This individual has connections in Moscow's criminal underworld."

"So he's what, a mob boss?"

"He is a mob boss the way a farm tractor is a car. So sort of."

Jake had no idea what Kaspov meant by that, but it wasn't like he could be choosy right now. As long as he didn't run into Baba Yaga, that was fine with him.

The car stopped in front of a rundown apartment building that Jake recognized as sitting just outside the border of Viper's alley. It looked identical to the building where Baba Yaga's opium den was.

"Odd place for a mob boss."

"Like I said, he is not exactly a mob boss."

Kaspov led Jake to a door protected by a steel grate and a massive doorman who looked like he could crumple the steel grate into a ball if he wanted to. He glared at Jake, but when Kaspov spoke to him, he nodded and opened the door for the two of them to pass.

The interior was far nicer than the exterior. Well, far cleaner, anyway. The paint was faded and chipped, and only about half the floor retained its linoleum tiles, but it was well-lit, and there were no strangers lying around in a drug-filled haze.

Kaspov led Jake to an office and knocked on the door. "Mikhail. I have a friend for you."

"I doubt he is a friend," a thickly accented voice called back. "But he is enemy of my enemy. That is good enough for now. Come in."

Jake walked in and stifled a cough. The room smelled heavily of incense burning in two separate bowls on either side of a wide pine desk. Behind the desk, a hugely fat man of around sixty sat with two scantily clad girls who couldn't have been more than twenty leaning on his shoulders. He whispered something to them, and they moved away. One of them looked Jake up and down hungrily as she headed for the door, but Jake got the impression the move was practiced rather than genuine.

Not that it mattered. That wasn't what he was here for.

"So," Mikhail said. "The old wolf has finally gone mad."

"What has Kaspov told you?"

"Everything. I hope." He chuckled at Kaspov. "Nikolai Ivanovich has kidnapped your President's daughter and tried multiple times to assassinate him. He suspects she is being held in a military bunker of some sort. He has given you an undisclosed amount of time to create a plan to deliver your President to him in exchange for her release. Is that everything?"

"Everything we have so far."

"Good. Then I am up to speed. Now let me return the favor.

"Nikolai Ivanovich is a brilliant man. I hate him, but even I can admit that he is brilliant. He is a chess master in both the literal and the figurative sense. Do you know what the point of chess is, Mr. American?"

"To take the king."

"No! That is the *end* of the game, but it is not the point of the game. The *point* of chess is to control the board. You see, the way to win is to limit the options your opponent has while maximizing the options you have. People who are new to chess play like you—to win. People who are masters play to control. Their goal is not to take the king but to take away their opponents' options. By hemming them in and forcing them

86

to make only the moves you want them to make, you can determine the outcome of the game. You can decide not only *if* you'll win, but *how* you'll win and how soon.

"Nikolai is, at this moment, impressed by you, angry with you and afraid of you."

Jake frowned. "Of me? Why?"

"Because you've taken his options away. He tried to have your President shot, and rather than move him somewhere vulnerable, you moved him out of harms' way. He tried to poison your president, but you saw through the gambit and took his queen. He tried to have your President stabbed at great risk to his rook, but you moved your king out of harms' way once more, and he has had to satisfy himself with threatening your queen."

"But I didn't move the President. He just moved out of the way."

"Nikolai doesn't know this. He thinks you've simply outsmarted him every step of the way. But now he believes he's outsmarted you. He's threatened your queen and put you in a position where you feel you must put your king in jeopardy to rescue her."

The portly old agent leaned forward, his smile vanished. "You must *not* offer up your king! Not even as bait! If you do, he will take him, and you will lose the game. Stall him. Force him to stay in check so his attention must be on defense, not offense. The moment you acquiesce to his demands, even as a ruse, you have lost. Keep him on his back foot and find a way to free your queen. You are in a race against time right now, American. Your best bet is not to win this race but to create more time."

Jake frowned. Up until that very second, his plan had been to use the President as bait. Not really, since he would be surrounded by agents, but he did plan to lure Nikolai in. Now Mikhail was warning against that very strategy.

"I will reach out to my contacts to see if I can locate your queen," Mikhail said, "but I can promise nothing. Nikolai is sly as a fox and venomous as an adder. He may outsmart me one more time. But"—he grinned again—"if he doesn't, then I would welcome the opportunity to turn the tables on him."

"Why are you doing this?" Jake asked. "Not to sound ungrateful for the help, but why do you hate him so much?"

"Because. He thinks he is smarter than me."

Jake stared at Mikhail in disbelief, laced with mild contempt. The old agent grinned, revealing rotting yellow teeth, and laughed at Jake's expression. "I wouldn't expect you to understand, agent. Only to accept my help regardless of my motives."

Jake had no choice after all. "I will. Thank you."

CHAPTER SIXTEEN

Kaspov was uncharacteristically silent on the drive back to the Kremlin. He scowled, his lips pushed forward pensively as the driver smoothly navigated the crowded city streets.

Jake didn't feel much of an urge to strike up conversation either. He played back the conversation with Mikhail in his mind, but no matter how many times he repeated it in his head, he didn't feel good about it.

Both Mikhail and Kaspov had advised him not to give ground to Nikolai. Topaz had confirmed this advice before even going to see Mikhail.

Jake understood that advice. From the perspective of a Secret Service agent, it was not only sound advice but the only option. The United States did not negotiate with terrorists. Full stop. Period. No matter what.

It didn't matter that Sheila was in the clutches of a mad genius bent on overthrowing the United States. It didn't matter that the only way to save her was to give up the President, or at least act like he was giving up the President so he could convince Nikolai to stick his neck out. He couldn't give Nikolai even the slightest chance to get what he wanted.

Except it did matter. Because that was the woman he loved. That was Sheila. That wasn't just anyone. It was the woman he was supposed to spend his life with, the woman he was supposed to have children with.

Three years. Three goddamned years. God, that's all he wanted.

It hurt more because he had seemingly defeated Trident. Until Bard, Drew, and Dalton were in prison, he wouldn't consider them truly defeated, but he had beaten them badly enough that they now lay dormant. He had thought before that if he defeated Trident, there would be no one left who could truly threaten the President.

Instead, his worst fear had come true. By Nikolai's own admission, Trident's actions had emboldened him. How many more waited in line to try their luck after him?

Jake sighed and ran his hands through his hair. God, he hated this.

Kaspov guessed correctly at the root of Jake's worry. "You must stay strong, Special Agent. I promise you, Nikolai will not hurt Sheila.

Not unless he is truly convinced he cannot use her. Do not let your fear rule you. Play smart."

Easy for you to say. "You don't think I should bait him like we originally talked about?"

"Not after talking to Mikhail. He is right, Nikolai is too clever. We cannot let him get close. We cannot count on another stroke of luck like the one we had earlier this morning. We must play hardball with him. Tell him we need assurances. Tell him we don't trust him, and we won't play his game. Perhaps you can say that your superiors refuse to cooperate so he thinks your hands are tied. But Mikhail is right. He must never know where the President is.

"I'll do my best."

"That's not good enough, Jake."

The use of his first name surprised Jake. He looked up to see Kaspov smiling at him. The FSB agent looked old and tired for the first time in Jake's memory. "Ours is not a job you can fail at. Believe me when I tell you, you don't want a failure like that on your conscience. You will succeed. You will not try, you will not do your best. You will succeed. You must."

Jake nodded. "All right."

The car pulled in front of the Kremlin. Jake got out, and the car sped off. He made his way to Jess, who sat in the Secret Service vehicle, watching him intently.

"Did you get anything useful?" she asked.

He shook his head. "Another ally. An old enemy of Nikolai's who wants in on the manhunt. Other than that, just a repeat of what we already know and more advice not to give in."

"That sounds like good advice."

"It is."

"So we'll follow it. Right?"

"Right. Yes, Jess. I won't betray my country. Just give me a break if I'm a little pissed off at the situation."

"I have given you a break," she said gently, "but you still need to be able to handle this."

Jake sighed. "I know. I will."

She put a hand on his shoulder and squeezed softly. "She'll be okay, Jake. We've always won before."

"Even Muhammad Ali lost eventually."

"But Rocky Marciano didn't. You know why? Because he never stopped. He ran ten miles a day, every day, even on Christmas and his birthday. He never drank or smoked, and he trained for hours every morning and every afternoon. He dedicated every aspect of his life to boxing, and because he did, he was able to beat people he shouldn't have had a chance with. He won forty-nine professional fights, and most of them weren't close. That's because he never stopped. So *you* don't stop. You can take a beating just like he could. You can keep going when other people give up. Hell, you were dying of a virus, a stab wound, a beating and a gunshot, and you still beat St. Clair and rescued Sheila the first time she was captured. You can do this, but only if you believe you can and only if you don't stop. Okay?"

Kaspov, Topaz and Mikhail had all tried to encourage Jake, but only Jess's words had an effect. Jake didn't know who Rocky Marciano was but knowing that someone else out there had managed to spend an entire career never slowing down even for a minute inspired him.

He could do it. One more fight. One more battle.

His phone rang. A private number. Jake had a feeling he knew who it was.

"Mercer."

"Time's up, Agent. What do you have for me?"

Jake took a deep breath. He was about to make a huge gamble. If it didn't pay off, then he could be putting Sheila's life at risk. "I'm afraid my hands are tied, Nikolai. I've spoken to my superiors. They will not agree to give the President's location to you."

A pause. "Why would you tell your superiors of this? The deal was between us. Of course they would not sacrifice the President. Were you planning to bait me?"

"Yes."

This was it. The risk. The gambit. Nikolai's reaction now would tell Jake whether it was worth it.

A longer pause. "You are being honest with me. That is interesting. I assume you have a reason for being so forthcoming. Or do you simply not care if I murder your woman?"

"I'm being forthcoming because I want to have a frank conversation with you. Here's the problem with your plan, Nikolai. You assume that because I'm the Chief of Security ,I can make decisions regarding the President's movements. I can't. He goes where he wants to go, and I arrange protection. If I want to suggest that he go somewhere else, he has to approve it. He didn't approve it, and I reached out to my superiors and explained the situation. My thought was that they would agree to lure you out and offer the President as bait. Then, as soon as we had Sheila in custody, you would be arrested or killed. Or, if there was no way to accomplish that, then I would sabotage the mission, give you the President, and take Sheila. I would suffer grave consequences for that, but at least she would be safe.

"They didn't go for it. No changes. Not only that, but they know that I'm in love with Sheila, so I've been replaced."

"You've been *replaced?*"

"Yes. I'm no longer making active decisions regarding the President's security."

This pause was long enough that Jake thought he had lost Nikolai, When the terrorist came back, he was calm once more.

"You are lying to me, Jake. Very clumsily. I know more about you than you think I do. Your superiors allow you full discretion when you work, and they've allowed you to exercise that discretion to shocking degrees in the past. If you told them that you needed to use the President as bait to save his life, they would believe you. You are trying to trick me to give yourself more time to find me and attempt a rescue without giving me what I want. No doubt you have taken some advice from people more experienced than you in this game.

"You are a bad liar, but you have called my bluff. You are right, or rather, your friends, whoever they might be, are right. I will not kill Sheila."

Jake felt an automatic flood of relief, but he knew better than to trust it. "What will you do?"

"I will hurt her."

Jake's blood froze. "If you touch her, I'll—"

"What? Kill me? Hurt me? I've already told you I don't care about myself. Tell your partner to answer my call."

The laptop beeped to indicate an incoming call. Jake reached for it, but Jess caught his hand and shook her head no. Jake slowly pulled his hand back, but when he heard Sheila's voice over his own phone, he reached forward and accepted the call.

Sheila was crying, "No! No, please!" as the masked man from earlier approached her with a meat cleaver.

"Nikolai!" Jake cried. "Listen! I can give you what you want! I just need more time!"

"You have it."

"Please don't hurt her! I'm doing my best!"

"You are. But not to help me."

"Nikolai! This is the President of the United States! It's not that simple!"

"It must become simple."

The masked man brought the cleaver down, severing the rope around Sheila's wrists. Sheila began beating on him with her fists, weeping and writhing in her chair.

The masked man shrugged off the blows and deftly caught one of her wrists. She shrieked and scratched at him. When her fingers drew blood, the masked man casually lifted his hand and backhanded her across the face. Her head whipped around, and she gasped and slumped forward, nearly knocked unconscious by the blow.

The masked man grabbed her wrist and pulled her hand forward again. Sheila began to fight once more, but the blow had rendered her weak, and the masked man had no trouble pressing her fist to the table in front of her and spreading her fingers so the ring finger was extended.

"Nikolai!" Jake screamed. "Stop it!"

"This time, she only loses a finger. Next time, she will lose something else. I'm not sure what yet, but it will be more painful than a finger."

The masked man lifted his cleaver. Sheila shrieked and lifted her other hand to block the knife, but she was a slender, petite woman, and the masked man was massive and thickly muscled.

"I'll kill you!" Jake screamed. "I'll kill you slowly! You hear me? I'll make it last, you bastard!"

The cleaver fell. Sheila screamed, and Jake's mind tore in two. The masked man released Sheila's arm. Gasping, retching and shrieking, she cradled it to her chest, then stared in horror when she realized what had just happened. She screamed again, then her eyes rolled back in her head, and she fainted.

The masked man picked up the finger and lifted it to the camera. Jess retched and whispered a choked, "Oh God."

Jake pressed his palms to his temples, his eyes refusing to accept what he had seen but unable to look away.

"This was your doing, Agent. You had a chance to save her. You didn't take it."

"You fuck! I'll—"

He heard a click as Nikolai hung up. Screaming with rage, he threw his cell phone against the car's windshield. The bullet proof glass didn't so much as crack, but his phone shattered. Jake knew that was a problem, but it was one he would deal with later.

Right now, he could only scream.

CHAPTER SEVENTEEN

"We can't tell the President," Jess said.

"No," Jake agreed. "We can't."

The two of them were back in front of the Kremlin. Both held half-full coffee cups. Jess's sandwich was half-eaten. Jake had eaten his in five minutes, mostly to keep his hands busy.

He had failed. He had promised to protect Sheila, and he had failed. She had gotten hurt because of that asshole Nikolai, and he hadn't stopped her.

He should have followed his own plan. He should have tried to bait Nikolai. He could have rescued Sheila, and he could have stopped the terrorist. He should never have listened to Kaspov.

"He wouldn't have brought Sheila," Jess said, guessing Jake's thoughts. "He would have lied to you, and when he found out you lied to him, we'd be in the same place right now."

"I could have given myself more time," Jake said. "I could have earned an extra day to find her if I had told him that I was giving him the President tomorrow."

Jess didn't reply to that. After a moment, she reached into her pocket and handed him a burner phone. "I activated it with the same number as your old one. Just in case."

Jake took a deep breath and put the phone in his pocket. "Thank you."

God, the way she screamed.

"It's not the end of the world, Jake. We know now that he won't kill her."

"But we know he *will* torture her."

"I know. But she'll survive this. Losing a finger is hard, but it's not nearly as hard as it could be."

"That was the ring finger on her left hand. She'll spend the rest of her life knowing it's gone. When I have to put the ring on the wrong finger when I propose, she'll know. She'll always know, and she'll always know that it was me who caused her to lose it."

"Enough of that," Jess said sternly. "We're not doing this. It was a terrorist who did this, not you."

"Yes, but—"

"No buts. Time to man up, Marine. Sorry to be this harsh, but we don't get to feel sorry for ourselves. He's clearly desperate, and he just as clearly is dependent on you to give him another opportunity to get to the President. He's playing on your emotions because that's all he has right now. Remember that."

"So what? We keep resisting him until he kills her out of spite because he can't get to the President?"

Jess pursed her lips. "I wish I could tell you something to make this better. I really can't."

Jake sighed and buried his face in his hands. He forgot about the coffee cup, and it burst open, spilling the hot liquid on his hand and thigh.

"Goddammit!" he cried. "Fuck!"

The pain wasn't bad at all. It was the emotional strain that caused him to cry out.

"Get a hold of yourself, Jake," Jess barked. "I can't do this without you."

"Fuck." He ran his hands through his hair. "All right. You're right. I know. Sorry."

"Listen, you have people looking for him, okay? Odds are, they'll find him. And at some point, Nikolai *will* have to make a move other than trying to bully you into making the move for him. I may not be a grandmaster, but I know that you can't win a chess game with defense only."

"The problem is that he might kill Sheila out of spite before he makes his move. If he really doesn't care what happens to him, then he won't care that I've threatened to kill him. He'll just kill Sheila, and then move on the President while I'm an emotional wreck."

"Don't take this the wrong way, Jake, but you're far more of an emotional wreck now than you would be if Sheila died. Right now, you still have something to lose. If you lose that something to lose, you'll be a being of pure rage." Jake met her eyes, and she said, "Yeah, I know it sounds silly, but it's true. You'll be angry and heartbroken, but you'll be focused again. Right now, you're not focused, and that's exactly where Nikolai wants you. He'll string this out as long as he can."

"Wonderful. So she keeps getting hurt."

"Jake, what do you want me to say?" Jess snapped irritably. "This is the life you chose."

"It's not the life Sheila chose. It's the life Bryan chose for her."

"My point is that there's nothing we can do to eliminate risk. We can mitigate it, but risk still exists, and this time, the bad thing happened before we could stop it. I'm sorry, Jake. I really am. But being pissed off and heartbroken and desperate and... and out of control like you are now isn't helping. This is the first time I've seen you this broken. It scares me."

"Well, I can't just snap my fingers and be happy-go-lucky again."

"Then be a Marine again. Forget about being a Secret Service agent. If she was in combat with you and she lost your finger, would you freak out and talk about how shitty it is that she got hurt and you couldn't stop it? Or would you keep fighting until the source of that shot was dead so that the next bullet didn't end up in her head instead of her hand? Look, I can shout at you all day long, but the bottom line is you know what you need to do. It's up to you to actually do it."

Jess's phone buzzed. "Hey, Dawson. Understood." She looked at Jake. "Yeah, he's with me. He's... maintaining." Her shoulders tensed a little. "No, no news. We have contacts looking, but there's nothing concrete yet. All right. We're ready whenever you are. He's going to come back to the hotel with us for now, but if we get a real lead, he'll be out following it. How did the summit go? Well, that's good news, at least. You can give us a full update later. Let's get the President back home. No, same hotel. Lightning shouldn't strike the same place twice, especially since the place is crawling with cops and security. All right. Let me know when you're in your vehicle."

She hung up and said, "Summit's over for the day. Dawson says good news, and the President is a little more relaxed. Still terrified, but he has confidence that everything will be okay." She met Jake's eyes. "You should too."

The convoy headed back for the hotel. Jess took over randomizing the route, taking them on a twisting journey through Moscow's crowded government district. At several points along the journey, Jake noticed FSB agents watching them. Kaspov had clearly beefed up his agency's presence in the area in response to the increased threat. That should have comforted Jake, but seeing their stony faces, he felt like a bug under a microscope.

It's not about you. It's about the President. He's your primary responsibility. You're winning as long as he's alive and safe.

But the sacrifice he would have to make... the sacrifice the President would have to make.

They reached the hotel, and Jake joined the others as they quickly led the President through the heavily guarded lobby and up the equally heavily guarded stairwell. When they reached the President's suite, they waited outside for ten minutes while Dawson and another agent searched it thoroughly. When they let the President inside, Jake saw that Carrie was sitting on the couch in the living room. He stopped a minute, unsure if he should let Bryan inside.

But when Carrie saw her husband, she showed no anger. Her lower lip trembled, and she burst into tears. Bryan was instantly at her side, his arm around her. He held her while she wept, saying nothing, only comforting her as they both mourned their missing daughter.

Jake wanted to tell them that everything was okay. He wanted to reassure them that he would find Carrie and bring her back to them unharmed.

But he couldn't. She was already harmed.

He left the two of them in their suite and headed to Jess's office. When the door closed, Jess said, "I made a map of the known military installations around Moscow and organized them into five tiers of likelihood. There are a lot of them, but I figure this will help Kaspov and Moscow Police adequately distribute their resources."

Jake felt a spark of hope. "Thank you, Jess. This is good. Get them this information."

"Already did." She smiled at him. "See? There's more of us than there are of him. He's going to lose, and we *will* get Sheila back. You can count on it."

Jake wasn't sure if he could, but he knew he could count on Jess to do everything in her power, and that was quite a lot. "Thank you again. And I'm sorry. I know I wasn't what I needed to be today."

"You don't have to apologize. I get it. I was only hard on you because, well..." she shrugged.

"I get it. I need you to be hard on me when I'm out of line like this. I can't let my fear overcome my common sense."

"Bold of you to assume you had common sense in the first place."

He chuckled, and just that brief amount of laughter was enough to lift his spirits. He didn't feel guilty for laughing. On the contrary, if he could laugh, then it meant he hadn't given up. He still had hope, and if he had hope, then he could succeed.

His phone buzzed, and he recognized the number as the one Mikhail had given him. He answered quickly, heart beginning to pound once more. "Mercer."

"American! Well played. I would have cautioned against involving the local police, but your gambit has worked! You have flushed your rabbit out of his hole! Or rather, *her* hole. I doubt the jackrabbit is with her."

"Are you saying you found Sheila?"

"I am staring at her right now. My instincts were spot on. Nikolai is doing exactly what I suspected he would do."

Jake's heart leapt. "Where is she?"

"She is on the river. Or rather, she is right by the river, but she soon will be in the river."

"Can you get to her?"

"I assume you don't mean me personally, since I am likely to kill myself simply descending this hill. Unfortunately, I cannot send someone for her either. She is under heavy guard. She appears to be drugged unconscious. She is being carried from the bunker to a boat. It seems Nikolai has caught wind of your plan to infiltrate each possible military location, and he's moving her to avoid being caught with his pants down. Pardon the phrase, I don't mean that literally.

"Where on the river?"

"I'll send you the coordinates. I would advise you not to come alone, but Americans will be cowboys! Good luck, American. And if you do see Nikolai, please kill him for me."

"You have my word on that."

He hung up and turned to Jess. Before he could speak, she said, "Already on it. I'll track you on this map, and just for good measure, I'll get Kaspov on the line too. Maybe he can send some backup since I imagine you'll be too impatient to wait."

"Got that right."

Jake's phone buzzed. He quickly fed Mikhail's coordinates into Jess's laptop. Then he rushed from the room.

Hold on, Sheila. I'm coming.

CHAPTER EIGHTEEN

"She has not yet left," Kaspov said in Jake's earpiece. "They are loading one more boat with supplies and ammunition. Wherever they are taking her, they intend to keep her there for a long time. That should encourage you, no? He clearly does not plan to kill her yet."

"If things go well, he won't be able to kill her," Jake replied.

Jess had put Kaspov onto the line with Jake so he could talk to the Russian Agent via his earpiece. The bunker Mikhail had identified was along the Moskva river and was ten minutes from the hotel. Jess had given Jake's license plate to the Moscow police, so he was able to ignore traffic laws and reach it in seven.

The moment he reached the bank opposite the bunker, he saw the boats. There were three of them. The one in the front had a machine gun mounted on a tripod. The one in the rear had a gun as well and also carried several pallets of cargo.

The boat in the middle was larger than both of the other two combined. Jake counted two machine gun emplacements along with armor and a radar warning receiver. Nikolai's security firm afforded him some impressive toys.

He gunned the motor of the vehicle and sped toward the dock. "Which boat is Sheila on?" he asked.

"The middle one," Kaspov confirmed. "She was taken belowdecks. Be careful. She will be under heavy guard."

"I will."

That became the least of Jake's worries a moment later when the boats saw him coming. They sped off, the last terrorist sprinting toward the water and doing a flying leap onto the rear boat.

"Dammit!"

"Look for a dock marked with an official logo. It should have a gray launch with an outboard motor. River police use it as a chase vehicle."

Jake slammed the brakes, and the vehicle skidded to a stop just before the docks. He looked around and quickly saw the boat Kaspov was referring to.

He jumped out of the vehicle and sprinted toward the launch. Already, Nikolai's men were well ahead of him.

He jumped into the boat and quickly began untying it from the dock. The cord was knotted well, and it took Jake a minute to get it undone. When he looked up, he could see the rear boat only as a distant speck. He estimated they were already three miles ahead of him.

He pulled the cord on the outboard motor. It sputtered.

"Dammit! Not now!"

"Press the red button on top of the motor," Kaspov said. "That will prime it with fuel."

Jake found the button and pressed it. This time, when he pulled the cord, the engine roared to life. Jake quickly braced himself and pulled the throttle lever. The front of the boat lifted sickeningly, but the vessel steadied and quickly accelerated out of the dock. Jake narrowly missed three other boats as he pulled into open water, but finally, he got the boat heading in the right direction.

As soon as he was headed toward the now barely visible terrorists, he opened the throttle all the way. The boat shot forward, bouncing along the water.

"Slide forward a few feet," Kaspov said. "You must balance yourself."

"How can you see me?"

"I can tell the boat is not moving as fast as it should because of the red dot on your partner's screen."

"You're in the hotel with her?"

"She has shared her screen with me. Do you want to ask about me, or do you want to focus on what you are doing?"

"Right."

Jake inched forward until the bow of the boat lowered, and the craft moved steadily. Jake felt his speed increase, and slowly but surely, the specks of the distant boats grew closer and closer.

The light was fading fast, though. If he couldn't see them, then he would lose them. The boat had a spotlight on the front, but Jake couldn't reach it without letting go of the throttle.

Thinking quickly, he removed his belt with his free hand and tied it around the throttle lever. He held the other end and inched forward until he could switch the spotlight on. The beam cut a wide arc into the night ahead, and Jake returned to the throttle.

His pants were sagging, but he managed to put his belt back on as the distance between him and the terrorists slowly waned.

He closed to about a quarter mile when the lookout on the rear boat noticed him. He pointed at Jake, then ran to the machine gun.

Shit.

Jake yanked the rudder to the left just before the gun opened fire. The boat lifted high on its right side and nearly capsized before it righted and sent Jake flying for the bank. He quickly threw it the other way, and the nose spun around. The craft slowed, stopped, then bounced over its own wake, narrowly avoiding another barrage of machine gun fire as it sped back to the middle of the river.

"What are you doing?" Kaspov shouted. "I thought you were a Marine!"

"I was! We don't sail in the Marines."

"What?"

"We ride boats. We don't drive them."

Kaspov sighed. "How is it that you won the Cold War? Be gentle with the rudder. You will tear the boat apart, yanking it like that!"

"Well, their fifties might tear the boat apart before I get a chance."

Jake ducked under another barrage and heard the rounds bore into the water behind him.

"Hold on," Kaspov said. "I may have an asset in the area that can help with the guns."

"I'll take all the help I can—"

Jake twisted the rudder to the left again, only just remembering not to pull it all the way. Still, the boat came up high on the right for a second before righting.

The zigzagging caused Jake to lose ground. The terrorists were now a half mile away. He wouldn't catch them as long as those guns were active."

"Kaspov? I could really use a solution for those weapons."

"On its way. Fall back to a mile and a half away."

"Fall back?"

"Unless you want to get shot by an anti-materiel rifle, yes. You can't sail, so I'd rather you not rip your boat apart trying."

"All right," Jake said. "I'm doing my best."

"Fuck your best. Fall *back!*"

"I am!"

Jake turned the rudder to the right, stopping at forty-five degrees. The boat didn't come up as high this time, and it actually accelerated faster, easily avoiding the burst of machine gun fire.

"I'm doing better on the turning."

"Good for you! I'll leave a sticker on your homework. Have you fallen back?"

Jake pushed the throttle lever back until he saw the distance between himself and the terrorists increasing. "Okay. I'm about a mile back now."

Kaspov sighed. "Add a half mile to that, then hold that distance."

He spoke in the tone an exasperated parent might use talking to an unruly child. Jake would be offended, but he was too busy trying not to die.

Another burst of machine gun fire went his way, but at this distance, at high speed on the water, the machine gun was losing its accuracy. Jake found that by continuing to zigzag and altering the speed of his turns, he was able to easily avoid the gunman.

"Kaspov! How—"

A streak of fire flew across the water from somewhere on the right bank. Jake watched in shock as the boat at the rear of the convoy exploded in a burst of yellow fame. The hull flew into the air and fell upside down in three pieces onto the water.

"Long," Jake finished.

"Stay where you are," Kaspov warned. "The boat in front will turn around to take the rear boat's place. They will think that you do not have another rocket launcher. I do, a mile ahead."

Jake watched as the boat did indeed turn around and head his way.

And keep heading his way.

Shit.

"Kaspov, we have a problem. They're not holding an escort position. They're attacking me."

"Shit. Okay, try to evade. I will send the rocket launcher your way."

The boat closed to within a mile, and the fifty-cal opened fire. Jake swore and turned the rudder to the right, but three shells tore into the boat, and when the launch righted, water began bubbling up into the hull.

"I'm hit!"

"You or the boat?"

"It's a fucking M2, Kaspov! If I was hit, I'd be in pieces!"

"Oh, screw you! Two more minutes!"

Another burst of machine gun fire—much closer this time—tore the prow of Jake's boat off. The bow dipped toward the water, and Jake gunned the motor to lift the nose again. It lifted—too much. He pulled the throttle back, and it dipped again, holding just above the water.

Jake looked ahead and saw the terrorist boat nearly in front of him. He could see the bared teeth of the machine gunner as he aimed the rifle at Jake. Jake ducked just in time. He felt the heat of the rounds passing overhead as his boat passed the escort boat.

"Hey, your guys know to shoot the boat with the machine gun, right?" Jake said. "Because I just passed the baddy."

"They know. Your best bet is speed right now. Give it everything you have left. Try not to capsize."

Jake pulled the throttle. He was able to get about ninety percent without losing control, but the boat was taking on water fast. He wasn't sure how long he would be able to go on like this.

Dammit, he should have taken someone else with him. If he had someone to bail water while he drove, they could keep going. As it was, if he didn't reach Sheila's boat soon, he would lose her.

"Incoming, Jake!" Kaspov cried.

Another streak of fire headed from shore to the terrorist boat. Jake heard a cry and turned around to see the boat crew jump into the water just before their boat exploded. He saw the barrel of the M2 windmilling in the air. It gained impressive height before falling back to the water and landing with a wet thud.

Jake turned ahead and saw that he had gained considerable ground. He was now only a few hundred yards from Sheila's boat.

He gunned the motor again. The boat picked up speed, but the water was now four inches deep. Jake estimated that he had taken on almost forty gallons. The extra four hundred pounds of weight proved too much for the motor. Jake heard a grinding, then a thud as the drive gear shattered. The boat rapidly slowed, then settled.

"No!" Jake cried. "Dammit!"

He stood where he was for a long moment, watching helplessly as his boat sank. He finally jumped off the side and surfaced to watch helplessly as Sheila disappeared down the river.

CHAPTER NINETEEN

"He couldn't have gone too far," Kaspov said. He reached down and hauled Jake from the water onto the inflatable boat. "There is a coast guard vessel steaming our way. It is not fast, but it is heavily armed and has radar and sonar."

"We need air and ground support," Jake said. "He could dock the boat at any point along the river."

"Two rivers."

"What?"

"There are two nearby tributaries of the Moskva headed upriver. One is frozen and impassable for his vessel, but the other, the Istra, is navigable. It is twenty kilometers upriver."

"He could reach that in fifteen minutes."

"Yes. But not to worry. As I said, he cannot get far. I have contacted the Coast Guard. We will have other vessels on the Istra and further down the Moskva to cut him off. Also air support and ground troops waiting. We can still catch him."

Jake nodded and tapped his earpiece. "Jess?"

"I'm here. Did you link up with Kaspov?"

"Yes. We're in an RHIB heading toward a Coast Guard vessel. I need you to link up with Kaspov so you can have a birds' eye view of the situation." He turned to Kaspov, who nodded and gave a thumbs up, then spoke into his own radio. "Looks like he's getting that set up for you. Any..." He took a breath to steady himself. "Any contact from Ivanovich?"

"Negative. I'll let you know if we hear anything."

Jake sighed. "Please do."

He tapped his earpiece again to end the call and focused on his breathing as the boat neared the Coast Guard patrol craft. He knew that if he didn't rescue Sheila this time, Nikolai was going to hurt Sheila again, and probably worse than he did the first time.

They needed to rescue her. Dammit, they needed to rescue her now.

When the boat reached the Coast Guard vessel, Kaspov piloted past it and swung it around in a wide arc. The Coast Guard vessel was steaming at full speed upriver so as not to lose any more ground against the terrorists. Kaspov steered the boat up to the patrol craft's hull and matched its speed, expertly keeping the boat steady despite needing to pilot it through the larger craft's wake.

Two sailors threw ropes down to them, and Kaspov said, "Tie one rope to the bow and another to the stern."

Jake carefully made his way to each rope in turn. It was difficult for him to maintain balance on the boat as it bounced over the patrol craft's wake, but he managed to get each rope tied. "Okay!"

"Now sit down and hold on to the grab handles on the inside of the gunwale! They're going to lift us onto the boat!"

Jake complied, and a hydraulic winch began to drone, lifting the boat off of the ground. A moment later, they were on the deck. The two sailors quickly secured the boat to the hull while Kaspov led Jake into the patrol craft's bridge.

He issued terse commands in Russian to the vessel's skipper and listened a moment while the skipper replied. Then he turned to Jake.

"The helicopters have launched and will begin to scan the water in a moment. We cannot detect anything on the vessel's radar yet, but that is likely because we are at ground level, and the river bends frequently."

As if to illustrate his point, the vessel banked to the left as it navigated one of those bends.

"What's the likelihood that he's already put to shore?" Jake asked.

"Not high. We are still too near Moscow, and Moscow police are patrolling the area. He'll want to get somewhere rural and forested before he puts to shore. By he, I mean his men. As I said, I find it unlikely that he is with them right now."

"Yeah, I got that. I'm more concerned about where Sheila is at the moment."

"Of course. Stay strong, Jake. We will find her. There are many of us and few of them."

There were many of "us" and few of "them" when Eli Bard stormed the White House. There were many of "us" and few of "them" when Vincent St. Clair killed thousands in Paris with a virus. There were many of "us" and few of "them" when Hadad destroyed half of the Western Wall.

But dwelling on that served no purpose, so Jake only nodded. "Do you have weapons? My handgun's fouled from being in the water."

"Of course. Do you want a handgun or a rifle?"

"Both."

Kaspov smiled. "A man after my own heart." He turned to one of the sailors and issued a command. The sailor saluted and ran off to fetch Jake some weapons.

An officer sitting near the front of the bridge in front of a large radar screen said something to the skipper. The skipper passed the message along to Kaspov, and Kaspov told Jake, "The helicopters are scanning now. We should have a hit in a moment."

"What if we don't?"

"Then he has sunk the boat, and that means he has gone ashore."

Jake could only pray that hadn't happened.

A moment later, the sailor returned carrying a Grach pistol and a VKS sniper rifle. Jake was familiar with the weapons from his time as a sniper in the Marine Corps. Since he was assigned to deep penetration missions with the SEALs, he was trained to familiarize himself with enemy weapons in case it became necessary to take one from an enemy, or, more likely, face a sniper armed with the weapons. The VKS had a lower effective range than his M40 rifle but much greater penetration and stopping power with shells over ten times as heavy as the 7.62x51 NATO rounds. They would be strong enough to penetrate the enemy's body armor from one hundred meters.

He replaced his handgun with the Grach. It wasn't a perfect fit, but he was able to get the strap to hold the weapon in place. The rifle, despite firing a heavier round, was roughly the same weight as his old weapon, though the bullpup design felt a little awkward.

That wouldn't make a difference at the ranges Jake intended to use the weapon. He slung it over his shoulder and nodded at Kaspov. "Thank you."

The radar operator cried out excitedly, and Jake understood the message even before Kaspov told him, "We've found the vessel! It's on the Moskva. It's still traveling on the water. We have an air unit painting it as clear as day."

"How far ahead?"

"Ten kilometers. We will reach it in fifteen minutes."

"Good. Keep an eye on the boat, but don't engage as long as it remains on the water. I don't want to risk hurting Sheila."

"Understood."

The patrol craft sped forward as the skipper opened the throttles. The diesel engines thrummed powerfully, and the skipper issued orders. Sailors assumed battle stations, and through the window, Jake could see men take positions behind the boat's thirty-millimeter cannons. He prayed they wouldn't have to use the heavy weapons.

"I'm going to set up at the bow," he told Kaspov. "Call me on the radio if you need to tell me anything. Jess, can you set that up?"

"He's linked. Be careful, Jake."

Jake couldn't care less about himself right now, but he said, "I will."

He headed out of the bridge and rushed to the bow of the boat. The prow had a pintle for small arms. Jake quickly attached the VKS rifle and sighted the scope. The weapon's accuracy would be severely affected by the pitch and roll of the vessel, but again, Jake hoped to be well within the rifle's effective range by the time he actually fired it.

When they were five minutes away, Kaspov said, "They're putting to shore now. The craft is slowing and approaching the left bank. We will round the bend ahead in two minutes, and then we will see it."

"Can your helicopter hold them on the boat?"

"No. They are firing on it as we speak. At its current altitude, it is safe, but if it descends lower, it will not be safe."

Jake swore. "There's no way to fire out of the side door?"

"Not with an accuracy level that makes me comfortable with the President's daughter on board the vessel."

Jake's lips thinned. "Can this boat go any faster?"

"I'm afraid not."

"What about one of the inflatable boats?'

"By the time it's in the water, we will be nearly upon them. Stay calm, Jake. They cannot debark and flee before we arrive. They are only now pulling to a stop, and they need to transport a prisoner."

Jake wasn't sure he accepted Kaspov's assurances, but with no other choice, he was forced to wait until their boat reached them.

Three minutes later exactly, the boat rounded a bend, and Jake saw the vessel. He looked through his rifle's scope and saw eighteen men in body armor and armed with AK-12 rifles leaving the boat. One of the men carried a bound Sheila over his shoulder.

Jake checked his range. Nearly a kilometer out still. He couldn't fire.

"Kaspov, I see her. They're heading ashore now."

The enemy combatants saw the approaching guard vessel and broke into a run. An overeager sailor opened up with the thirty-mil, and Jake saw a half dozen terrorists shredded to pieces before Kaspov shouted a command, and the fire stopped.

The man carrying Sheila turned around and stared at the boat in alarm. Five hundred meters.

He shifted Sheila's weight and spoke into a radio receiver. Four hundred meters.

He turned and ran as fast as he could to a dense thicket of reeds along the bank. If he disappeared into that, Jake would lose visual. Three hundred meters.

At one hundred meters, Jake would fire. The boat still pitched sickeningly, but he had timed its rhythm and he was confident he could place his round without harming Sheila. Two hundred meters.

The man was about fifty meters from safety. Jake would have one, maybe two shots before he lost him. He took a deep breath and steadied himself, ignoring the rifle rounds that zipped past him as the terrorists returned fire.

One hundred fifty meters. One hundred thirty. One hundred ten.

Jake felt something hit his shoulder. He fell backward, hitting the deck hard before he realized what had happened. Then an explosion of pain rippled down his right arm.

They had a sniper. An enemy sniper had just hit him in his right shoulder. His trigger arm.

He couldn't fire his rifle.

"No!" he cried out. "Dammit!"

He started to his feet but dropped when another rifle round sailed past him. The boat lurched crazily, and Jake realized the helmsman had been shot.

"Jake! To me!"

Jake turned to Kaspov and saw the man rushing his way. "No!" he shouted. "Get down!"

Too late. A red hole opened in Kaspov's forehead, and a mist of blood, brain and bone flew out of the back of his head. He fell to the deck, lifeless.

"Goddammit!"

The boat lurched the other way as the skipper took control of the helm. Another rifle round entered the bridge, but the skipper kept low, and the round buried itself in the bulkhead behind him. Jake rolled to his stomach and pulled his rifle down with his good arm so he could look through the scope.

Three hundred meters away, just at the limit of the patrol craft's spotlight, was Jake's old friend Andrew McNeill.

Jake's eyes widened. After being dishonorably discharged from the Marine Corps, Drew had joined Bard and was now Trident's second in command. Trident was involved in this after all.

Drew sighted calmly and fired. Jake heard a cry as the sailor manning the port cannon fell to the deck, blood gushing from his side.

The starboard cannon turned toward Drew. Drew flicked his rifle that way, then swore and jumped just before a volley of thirty-millimeter shells obliterated his tree stand.

Jake lifted himself over the rail to see a van speeding away along a rough dirt road. He recognized it as the van Sheila's kidnapper had used to escape the hotel.

He caught a glimpse of Sheila's frightened eyes staring out of the back of the van before a hand pulled her roughly down.

The skipper, recognizing that the target was lost, pulled the vessel back to the center of the river. Once more, Jake could only stare helplessly as the love of his life was taken out of his reach.

CHAPTER TWENTY

"You lost her again."

The President's tone wasn't accusatory or even angry. It only expressed disappointment and a touch of resignation that disturbed Jake more than any amount of anger could have. His brows were furrowed, and his lips were set in a dark frown, but his shoulders slumped, and his breathing came almost reluctantly, as though it were a chore for him to continue.

Perhaps it was. Bryan had once joked with him that he was both the most powerful and least powerful man on Earth. His actions dictated policy across the globe as allies conformed and enemies reacted.

But when it came to keeping his own daughter safe, he could do nothing but wait and hope that other people could exercise the means to rescue her.

And Jake had failed. Again.

"Yes, sir," he said, hating the defeat in his own voice. "With help from Agent Kaspov, we tracked the fleeing terrorists to a bend in the Moskva river about thirty miles outside of the city, but unfortunately, the enemy was entrenched and prepare for our arrival. Agent Kaspov was killed, as were three crew members of the patrol craft we took to apprehend the terrorists and rescue Sheila. The enemy suffered ten casualties, but the survivors were able to flee in two modified UAZ vans. The FSB is continuing to scour the area, but at this time, we've been unable to locate the vehicles."

The President nodded. "Has he hurt her."

Jake resisted the urge to share a glance with Jess. "No, sir. We don't believe so."

"Don't lie to me, Jake."

Jake opened his mouth to do exactly that, but the accusation in Bryan's eyes stopped him. "Yes, sir," he said softly. "He... he removed one of Sheila's fingers."

The President's façade broke entirely. "Good God," he whispered, leaning forward and burying his face in his hands. "Oh God." He let his hands fall and stared over Jake's shoulder. His eyes were moist, but he didn't weep. Not yet. "I'm glad Carrie isn't here."

The First Lady had gone to bed early. Aside from Jess, Jake and the President, there was only Dawson and his ever-present security detail.

"Why?" Bryan asked.

"Sir?"

The President sighed and rubbed the bridge of his nose. "Why did he cut off my daughter's finger? Just to show he was serious?"

"Yes, sir. He…" Jake hesitated again, but there was no point in further lies. "He attempted to bargain with me for your life. He stated that if I gave him access to you so he could assassinate you, then he would return Sheila unharmed."

"So this is the same person who was lying in wait on the original route to the Kremlin, and the same person who tried to poison me."

"Not the exact same person, but the person we believe is responsible for every attempt so far."

"Is he connected to the people who killed Gene?"

"Gene?"

"The Ambassador to China. Same people?"

"We believe so, sir."

"Trident?"

Jake recalled Drew's almost smug expression as he shot Kaspov. He recalled how helpless he felt with a rifle but no arm to shoot it with. His injured shoulder throbbed despite the painkillers Jess had insisted he take.

But he hadn't shot Jake dead. Why not? Had Bard ordered Drew to keep him alive?

The President waited for an answer to his question, so Jake put that thought aside for later. "Yes, sir."

Bryan slumped forward again. He shook his head and began to laugh. "God, these assholes really have a hardon for me, don't they?"

Jake didn't respond.

"Is there a reason you didn't try to bait him?"

"Bait him?"

"Enough acting stupid," Bryan snapped.

Jake sighed. "The United States doesn't negotiate with terrorists."

"Don't be an idiot. We negotiate with terrorists all the time. This entire fucking summit is negotiating with terrorists. Answer my question."

"We believed—and still do—that such a strategy would ultimately prove ineffective. We don't believe that Nikolai—the terrorist responsible—would follow through with his end of the bargain. If we

112

attempted to deceive him, we would either lose her or lose both of you."

Bryan sighed and tapped the table with his finger. "Now that you've lost her again, what do you think he'll do to her? Do you think he'll kill her?"

"No, sir. She's the only leverage he has right now. If nothing else, we've demonstrated that we have the ability to hurt him. We flushed him out of his hiding spot, destroyed his equipment, and killed several of his men. We did this with the cooperation of the Russian government. He has no friends now, and he knows that. Without your daughter, there's nothing keeping us from going scorched Earth."

"But he'll hurt her again."

Jake didn't answer, which was all the answer the President needed. "Fucking hell." He stared moodily at the table a moment, then lifted his eyes to Jake again. "You know, I take them with me everywhere I go because I'm afraid if I leave them behind, Trident will come after them to hurt me. I figured as long as they were under the Secret Service's protection—my level of protection—they would be more likely to be safe than if they were left apart from me. When your agents betrayed us on Air Force One, I thought I had failed, but then you pulled another miracle out of your ass and somehow managed to get us home safely. I thought you were invincible. That was my mistake."

Bryan didn't mean that to sound as accusatory as it did, but it crushed Jake anyway. He lowered his gaze and said nothing.

"Don't tell me what happens to Sheila. It's taking all of my energy to keep going with this charade as it is. Just get her back—as much of her as you can—and I'll cope with the damage when I know she's safe. Or when this summit ends. Christ, I hate being President sometimes."

I don't blame you, sir.

The President stood and left the room without another word. Dawson and his team filed out after him. As he left, Dawson cast a sympathetic look on Jake's way. Jake wouldn't ordinarily want sympathy, but he'd take any form of encouragement he could get right now.

Jess looked at Jake, her eyes filled with worry. "Jake. It's Nikolai."

Jake's shoulders slumped. "Did he leave a message?"

Jess turned her laptop so Jake could see it. The screen was split. On the right side, Nikolai sat in a small but well-appointed office. On the left side, Sheila sat slumped in a chair in a much smaller room than earlier. Her hair was caked with leaves and dirt, and her clothes were stained from being carried through the water.

The massive man who had cut her finger off before stood to her right, holding a pair of gripper tongs. Jake's heart sank when he saw them.

"Agent," Nikolai said, his voice betraying the irritation that his calm face didn't show. "It seems you have more important things to do than talk to me. Perhaps you are still hunting for my operators and your precious President's daughter. You can call off that search. They are in hiding once more, and this time, your friends in the Security Bureau won't be able to help you.

"I must confess some admiration, both for you and for the FSB. I dismissed them as a hack agency unworthy of the legacy of the KGB from which they descended. I dismissed you as little more than a glorified bodyguard unsuited to the task of facing me. You have proven yourself far more capable than I expected. I normally scoff at aggressive offense, but when your opponent's defense is weak, such a play can be effective, and for you, it nearly was. Three times, you put me in check. Were it not for help from your old friend, I would have lost.

"However, I have managed thrice to elude you. I am now castled, and you are not well-placed to take my rook and expose me. Your gambit has failed. It's my move now."

The man with the tongs grabbed Sheila's hair and yanked it back. Sheila gasped, and the man quickly gripped one of her upper teeth with the tongs. Sheila cried out and tried to twist away, but the tongs held her like a vise, and she was unable to free herself.

"I read a study once," Nikolai said. "The study was to determine which part of a woman's body a man found most attractive. One might think the answer would be something vulgar or sexual: the breasts, the buttocks, the vagina, perhaps long legs or curvaceous hips.

"The answer, however, was shockingly chaste. Well, perhaps not chaste but certainly far more romantic than the prurient fantasies popularized by the pornography websites." Nikolai grinned at his camera. "It turns out that for most men, the sign of a truly attractive woman is a beautiful smile."

"You bastard," Jake whispered, "You bastard."

"I told you I would hurt her again if you didn't give me what I want, Agent. I told you that I would make her suffer. And so I will. You nearly caught me three times. So, I will take three of Sheila's top teeth.

She can correct this, of course, with veneers and caps, but the discerning eye will recognize the falsehood, much as the discerning eye can tell the difference between natural cheekbones and those that have been lifted or filled.

"I will take your woman's beauty, Special Agent, and soil it. Even if you get her back, you will know forever that I have taken something that can never be replaced."

He pressed a button on his computer and spoke in Russian.

Jess turned away and covered her ears. Jake didn't. He forced himself to watch and listen throughout the entire ordeal. Every scream of pain and despair seared itself into his mind. The blood that sprayed from her mouth burned its image onto his eyes. The choked sobbing that followed when it was over hammered itself onto his brain.

And with it, a promise.

I will kill you. All of you. Nikolai, Drew, Bard: I will personally watch all of you leave this world.

When it was done, Nikolai looked at the camera with an almost sad expression. "Such a pity. She truly was a lovely girl. Your move, Agent."

The message ended. Jake heard Jess retching behind him. He continued to stare at the screen as Jess vomited.

A few minutes later, Jess choked out, "Oh God," and sat straight. Her face was pale, and dark circles hung under her eyes. She looked warily at Jake, as though expecting him to fly into a rage and tear the room apart. They remained that way for several minutes. Finally, Jess asked, "What do you want to do?"

Jake took a deep breath and released it slowly. "Ensure that the President remains secure tomorrow. Keep in contact with Moscow Police and the FSB. And call Mr. Topaz. Kaspov is dead, and the FSB has proven to be ineffective at catching Nikolai. It's time to try another organization."

"Jake, shouldn't we…"

She didn't finish the thought, but Jake knew the question and answered it. "No. He's still lying. If we try to bait him, he'll learn of it and have Sheila killed somewhere far away where we can't reach her. The best bet is still to find him."

"What if we don't? What if we can't?"

Jake sighed. "Then I'll take full responsibility. I'll inform the President of Sheila's death, and I'll resign from the Secret Service and accept whatever prosecution the President and the Service deems necessary."

"Jake, it's not your fault. Don't blame yourself."

"It doesn't really matter whose fault it is. It's my responsibility. And I'm failing at it."

"Not yet. Don't give up hope."

Jake didn't bother arguing with her, but his hope had died watching Nikolai's smug face as his minion disfigured Sheila. All that was left to him was hate.

That was fine. He could use that.

Enjoy your victory, little spy. You'll pay dearly for it.

CHAPTER TWENTY ONE

"I won't lie, Jake. This is bad."

Mr. Topaz spoke with the same infuriating calm with which he always spoke, but that didn't dampen the seriousness of his tone. Still, Jake didn't need his help, realizing that this was a bad situation.

"I know that, Topaz. What I need to know is how to make it better."

Topaz didn't answer right away. He spoke with the two Secret Service agents over the phone, so Jake couldn't see him, but he imagined Topaz was tapping his fingers together in front of him, the only habit the CIA operative had that Jake would consider consistent.

"The issue is that the President won't leave Russia until Sheila is found. The other issue is that her kidnapping and the rather sensational time you had trying to recapture her is the number one story in the global news right now. As you might imagine, there are dozens of nations clamoring for Russia to be held accountable. Congress is already drawing up sanctions and the President's political opponents have intimated that if he refuses to agree to them, it's proof that he hates his daughter, hates America, loves Russia and wants the terrorists to win. I'm paraphrasing, of course, but I'm not exaggerating. I'm only using more blunt language than they are. The same pattern is repeating with minor variations across the Western world and in our eastern allies as well.

"Meanwhile, the Eastern world is decrying the thought that they could be responsible and demanding to know why Russian lives are being lost defending a foreign President's daughter. I don't know if you've paid much attention to local news in Moscow, but you might want to give it a glance. There are protests in the streets of Moscow, and the police have started to call for riot squads. You'll need to plan extra time to get the President to the Kremlin, and frankly, I wouldn't count on Moscow Police remaining vigilant for much longer.

"Even China's broken her silence. They're claiming that the President acted irresponsibly by bringing his family to this summit as though they were on vacation and not determining the outcome of several very volatile situations. They've announced that they 'stand by'

Russia's position and insist that Washington must be the one to make concessions or Western imperialism will gain too much ground.

"The short version of everything I just said is that whether you rescue Sheila or not—"

"When," Jake interrupted. "When we rescue Sheila."

"This summit will still be a failure," Topaz continued without acknowledging Jake's interruption. "The United States and its allies will not achieve their goals, and the rift between our countries will grow wider. Here's the real problem, Jake: Nikolai's goal isn't to assassinate the President. I'm not saying he won't welcome that if it occurs, but I'm saying it's not critical to his plan. He's not trying to kill the President, he's trying to push us into another Cold War, maybe even a hot one. And he's doing a damned good job."

He let those words hang in the air. Jake slumped back in his chair and wiped his brow with a shaky hand. "Dammit, I can only do so much. I just want to get Sheila back and the President through this meeting safely. I'm a Secret Service agent. I'm not a politician. I'm not a spy. I'm just a bodyguard."

"No one blames you, Jake. Least of all me. If anything, I blame myself. This is my sphere of responsibility, and I never saw Nikolai coming. I'm not telling you this because I think you should feel guilty, I'm just making sure you understand the problem here."

"I understand it, but how does that help me? How does it help us get Sheila back?"

"That *is* the problem. We can't rely on Russian help anymore. We need to find her ourselves."

"With what? We don't have the resources here."

"Relax. I still have resources. I can still look for Nikolai, and I'll bet you my job I can still find him. We just have to be patient."

"Patient? How can I be patient?"

"You don't have a choice."

Topaz wasn't angry when he said that, but he was far from sympathetic either. Jake slumped further in his chair. His shoulder throbbed, and knowing that he couldn't even fight effectively for at least another week killed him. It would be even longer before he could fire a rifle, and that killed him anymore. The fact that the bullet had landed in between his shoulder blade and the ball of his shoulder and not shattered either bone no longer seemed like a silver lining. The bullet had been removed and the wound bandaged, but even when he could take it out of the sling, his arm wouldn't be a hundred percent for another four weeks, possibly even longer.

"So let's look at the silver lining now that I've shown you how dark the cloud is. The FSB and Moscow Police might not be putting their best foot forward looking for Nikolai, but if there's one thing the Russians do damned well, it's putting so many boots on the ground that there's no way around them. Nikolai is stuck inside of a fifty-square-mile cordon, and that noose is tightening daily. Even if we just sit on our asses, he'll eventually be flushed out again."

"And he'll kill Sheila in the meantime."

"He will *not. Kill. Sheila.* The moment he does that, he becomes the bad guy. Russia becomes the bad guy, and global opinion shifts instantly. Sheila is a martyr, and the President is a hero for not backing down. China disappears into neutrality, and the Russian government loses all of its goodwill."

"So he continues to hurt her. That's not acceptable."

Topaz sighed. "Jake, I don't know what to tell you. Believe me, if I could wake up, snap my fingers and make everything better, I would, but that's not how this works. You're dealing with a very different kind of terrorist in Nikolai. He's a chess master, not a football player. He's not going to keep hammering you like Bard did. He's going to bait *you* to come after *him* and make *you* defeat yourself. The only way to stop that is to force him to chase you."

"So what do I do? I just wait?"

"Yes. You focus on keeping the President safe and let me play chess with him. This is my specialty. Give me the ball and do *your* job. Be a Secret Service agent and let the CIA operative handle the CIA work."

Topaz was right. Jake knew he was right. It was unquestionably the right decision.

But it meant doing nothing about the fact that the woman he loved was being tortured by a terrorist. It meant accepting that he wasn't able to help her and letting someone else do that. It meant waiting to hear that she was safe instead of making sure she was safe.

He leaned forward and pressed his palms to his temples hard enough that his head began to hurt.

"Jake? You there, buddy?"

"Yeah," Jake said. "I heard you. I'll do what you tell me to do. Just please let me know when you find her."

119

"Of course. You're also a Marine, and I'd rather you were the one storming the place guns blazing. I just need to point before you can shoot."

"Well, then get pointing."

"That's the spirit. Chin up, Jake. We can still win."

He hung up, and Jess said, "Anything I can do to help, I will. I'm on your side. You know that."

"Call Dawson and put us on conference call. We need to discuss the President's security tomorrow. And turn on the news. I don't need an English language channel, just anything with images that can get me an idea of what we're going to be facing in the morning."

Jess obliged, and when the TV blinked on, Jake immediately saw what Topaz was talking about. The image showed the hotel they were sitting in right now. Thousands of protestors stood outside behind a police cordon, shouting, waving signs and singing the Soviet National Anthem.

He looked out of his window, and he could see them. He had been so distracted that he hadn't thought to check before.

Not the Russian one. Topaz was right about that, too. Nikolai was bringing about a return to the Cold War, or at least helping the world along that path.

"Can we get an image of the other side of the building?" Jake asked.

Before Jess could reply, the image on the tv changed, showing thousands of protestors on the other side of the hotel as well. More images flashed, showing the Kremlin and the various streets surrounding it filled with chanting, marching protestors.

"Dawson here," the Agent's voice said over Jess's computer.

"Dawson, have you been keeping up with the news?"

"Not really. How bad is it?"

"Bad. It looks like the ground route might be compromised."

"Shit. Do we have another route?"

Jake sighed. "The only other route is the air route, and that requires FSB cooperation. They're… not very happy with us right now."

"We could play up the sympathy card. Stand for what Kaspov gave his life for: unity between our nations."

"Yeah, right now that reads like, 'act a fool like Kaspov did so that more Russians die.' Stupid question, but do we have any allied assets in the area?"

"I can answer that," Jess said, "but it's not the answer you want. I'm looking at news feeds from our allies' home nations, and it looks like every hotel where a Western delegate is staying is experiencing a similar volume of protests. The UK and Italian Parliaments as well as our own Congress is lobbying for the summit to end and for the heads of state to return home before something catastrophic happens." She lifted her eyes to Jake. "I hate to say it, but maybe that's not a bad idea."

"It's a non-starter whether it's a good idea or not," Jake said. "The President won't leave Russia without his daughter."

"Do we have any news on that end?" Dawson asked.

Jake's lips thinned. "I've turned the investigation over to Mr. Topaz of the CIA. We're not equipped to conduct a manhunt, less so now that our contact with the FSB is no longer here to help us."

Dawson sighed. "Okay. So the only way to the Kremlin is by ground, and we have thirteen of us plus the Counter Assault Team."

"I'm leaving Poole and Goering here," Jake said. "We need eyes in the hotel security room. I don't think we can count on building security to remain loyal to us."

"Okay, so eleven of us plus the thirteen members of the CAT. That's twenty-four. That's… well, it's not encouraging, sir."

"I don't want to assume that this is going to turn into a firefight. Ideally, we manage to get through this without one."

Dawson didn't respond right away. When he did, it was with some reluctance and a touch of guilt. "To be honest, sir, I think I need to turn this over to you. I don't think I have the experience to know how to handle this."

Jake nodded. "That's all right. I understand. Here are my thoughts. We publish the President's route, and we follow the route we publish. We tell Moscow police that we'll be traveling under armed protection from our Counter Assault Team. We tell them we'll be leaving for the Kremlin an hour early and will be returning by the same route."

Dawson's pause communicated the same shock as Jess's stunned look. "Sir… that's… wouldn't that be the same as announcing to our enemies exactly where we are?"

"Yes," Jake admitted, "but it will also give the protestors an outlet. We're letting them know exactly where they should be and what they can do. I know it seems counterintuitive, but by telling them where they can shout obscenities at the President while also making it clear that we're prepared to deal with anyone trying to harm the President, we can mitigate some of the unpredictability that protests like these cause. It's a gamble, but it's also our best bet."

Another pause. "I hate gambling."

Jake chuckled bitterly. "Yeah, me too."

Dawson sighed. "All right. I'll inform the security detail. Tell the CAT boys not to be too trigger-happy. They're still pissed about losing the President's daughter."

"I will. Thank you, Dawson."

He hung up and turned to Jess. "Think this'll work?"

"Do you want the honest answer or the encouraging answer?"

"You know what? Don't answer. I'm tired of second-guessing everything."

"Me too."

CHAPTER TWENTY TWO

It was one thing to see the protests on TV. It was quite another to be in the thick of them. On TV, the scope of the protests seemed massive. On the ground, it seemed endless.

It was the noise really that made things so intense. The crowd roared so loudly that Jake had to cover his left ear in order to hear his agents through his earpiece. His arm still throbbed in its sling, and without his firing hand, Jake felt almost naked in spite of the Grach pistol he still carried in his shoulder holster.

The Moscow Police held the cordon but made no attempt to stop or punish the debris hurled at the motorcade. Fruit, garbage and raw meat splattered against the windows of the vehicles, and the Combat Assault Team moved to block the motorcade with their own vehicles. When that angered the crowd, Jake ordered them back to their position.

The Moscow Police officers occasionally glanced at the motorcade. Jake could see the contempt written on every face. If they lost control of the crowd, they would make no attempt to regain it.

"How long until we reach the Kremlin?" Jake asked Jess.

"We have four miles to go," she informed him. "At this rate, we will arrive in one hour, which means we'll be there just in time."

"We need to park inside the structure."

"Yes, the FSB detachment at the Kremlin has already indicated that we're to park in the armored garage. If it makes you feel better, they at least sounded professional. That's a good sign, right?"

"It's a sign that they still don't want anything to happen at the Kremlin," Jake said. "It doesn't mean they'll fight to stop anything that happens outside."

A rock sailed through the air and smashed against the windshield. The bulletproof glass didn't even chip at the impact, but the loud thunk it made caused Jess to jump. Once more, the CAT vehicles began to flank the motorcade, but Jake ordered them back.

"Rocks won't hurt him. A crowd of thousands smothering us will."

"I understand that, sir, but if one of those windows breaks—"

"They're certified XSAPI. Unless someone has a fifty-cal, they're not going to break."

"They might have a fifty-cal. Or a rocket launcher. This is Russia, Mercer."

"Hold your position, Captain Munoz. That's an order."

Munoz sighed. "I will for now, sir, but if someone pulls a real weapon, I'm going to do what I have to do."

"You'll do as your instructed, Captain."

Munoz didn't respond. That wasn't good. Not only had Jake lost control of the situation with Nikolai and Sheila, but he was losing control of his team. If Munoz went off the reservation and started firing into the crowd, this entire scenario would collapse. He wondered if he should have left the CAT at the hotel.

They wouldn't have stayed, he thought. *Not with the threat this serious.*

The motorcade inched forward. From time to time, a Russian citizen broke through the crowd only for police officers to stop them. Once, Jake caught three officers throw a man to the ground and beat him savagely with their batons.

This wasn't good. This wasn't good at all.

Finally, they reached the Kremlin. Two stone-faced guards in military uniforms opened a steel-reinforced concrete gate for them to drive through. Rather than police in riot gear, the Kremlin was guarded with heavily armed members of the FSB. The crowd gave the building a wide berth, knowing that the federal agents wouldn't hesitate to fire their weapons if they deemed the protestors a threat to the security of the government.

They headed inside, and Jake noticed the CAT officers cast nervous glances at the FSB agents. *Keep it together, boys.*

They reached the entrance to the building, and the FSB commander stopped them, palm upraised. "No soldiers," he said in English. "Secret Service is fine, but no soldiers."

"We *are* soldiers," Munoz informed him. "Now out of my way before—"

"Munoz!" Jake barked. "Pull your men back to the vehicles."

Munoz met Jake's eyes with a glare, but he said, "Yes, sir," and did as he was instructed.

The FSB agent nodded once and ushered the President and his team inside. Jake and Jess waited outside.

"You are not coming?" The FSB officer asked.

"No, we'll wait in the car."

The officer's eyes narrowed. "You are the agent who led Kaspov to his death."

Jake chose not to argue, but he didn't acknowledge the accusation either. "I was with him when he died."

The officer nodded. Then he spit a wad of phlegm onto the ground near Jake's feet and looked over his shoulder, pretending not to see him.

Jake glared at the man a moment, but he was in no mood to argue. So, he turned and headed back to the van.

"Are you sure the President is safe in there?" Jess asked softly.

"I'm sure there's nowhere else to put him," Jake said.

They felt a little better inside the vehicles. That was entirely psychological, of course. The walls of the parking lot were cornered by fifty-caliber machine gun emplacements that would shred the motorcade vehicle's armor. The CAT vehicles moved to surround them, and this time Jake didn't protest, though he did tell Munoz to calm down when the M2 emplacements on top of the MRAPs turned to face the Soviet weapons.

Russian weapons. Not Soviet Weapons. Dammit, Jake is letting his own mind run away with him.

"I brought food and coffee," Jess said. "And there's a toilet in the back of the cab, so we can stay turtled up here the whole day."

"Is that supposed to be encouraging?"

"It encourages me. I don't like having guns pointed at me."

"You think I do?"

"You sure act like you do."

Jake sighed. "Can you get any kind of surveillance feed? I want real-time info on the situation outside."

Jess sighed. "Well, I can try, but without Kaspov here to help, I have to steal that information. Here's hoping that Kaspov was just unusually good at his job and no one else can crack my firewalls while I'm cracking theirs."

"Just do your best."

"You know, that never actually means do your best. It always means succeed or else."

"Well, succeed or else."

Jess glared at him. "I really hate you sometimes."

"Not sure how to help with that."

The day dragged on. Jake indulged in the sandwiches, water bottles and coffee Jess brought. Jess offered to share her potato chips, but he turned those down. Every five minutes, he asked for an update from outside. Every five minutes, he received the same answer. "Same as before. I'll tell you when things change."

Jake kept asking, though, and he kept playing through different scenarios in his head for the return drive to the hotel. He needed to keep his mind occupied on the President's safety. If he stopped for even one minute, his thoughts would turn back to Sheila, who was God-knows-where right now. At any minute, he expected a phone call from Nikolai telling him time was up and please enjoy this video of my friend beating Sheila to death. Topaz's assurances that he wouldn't kill Sheila weren't enough for Jake. Nikolai was unhinged. Unhinged people didn't behave logically, and if he felt pressure, he would behave even more erratically.

God, please keep her safe, he prayed silently.

***

On the way home, Jake was surprised to find that the crowd was significantly smaller than before. He was equally surprised to see them cheering rather than shouting.

He brought this up to Jess, who said, "Well, they're jeering, actually, not cheering. According to reports leaked from inside the summit, the day went pretty poorly for us. Russia went back on earlier promises to deescalate in Eastern Europe and pledged to commit more soldiers to their offensive against former Soviet nations. They've also warned that they will defend their allies in the Middle East with violence. The President, for his part, warned of more sanctions, and the Russian President laughed at him and said it was only a sign of Western weakness that we refused to commit our own soldiers to combat them."

Jake sighed. "Got it. Well, like you said earlier, politics isn't our job. Let's focus on the silver lining that the President is safer now."

"Safer *for* now is a more accurate way of putting it."

"Don't you start being pessimistic now that I'm trying to see the bright side of things."

"That's exactly why I'm being pessimistic. I don't have to carry you emotionally anymore."

Jake managed a chuckle, but his smile quickly faded.

"Hey, I didn't mean that," Jess said. "I was just joking. You know you can rely on me."

126

"I know I can. That just makes it even harder that this is something you can't fix for me."

Jess sighed. "Yeah. I know how you feel."

They reached the hotel and got the President up to his room. Understandably, he was very unhappy with the day's events. He looked far older than his fifty-eight years of age and walked with a stoop that Jake had never seen before.

Jake had read an article once that talked about how much being the President aged someone. It showed before and after pictures of Presidents at the start and end of their terms. Eight years typically resulted in a noticeable age difference, but it was clear that the Presidency accelerated that process significantly. Jake imagined it would be even more noticeable in Bryan's case.

If he even survived his Presidency. If they couldn't rescue Sheila...

No, he wouldn't let himself think that way. It was upsetting to have to rely on other people to do the work, but that didn't mean the work wouldn't get done. He had to trust that Topaz could play his part.

He said goodnight to Jess and started to walk to his room when his phone buzzed. When he saw Topaz's number, he turned around and motioned for Jess to enter her room. "Mercer."

"We got her, Jake."

"You found her?"

Jake was so shocked by the news that he stopped outside of the room, and Jess had to pull him in and shut the door to maintain confidentiality. Jake put Topaz on speaker and said, "Okay, you have me and Jess here. Go ahead.

"We found her in an underground bomb shelter within that cordon I told you about. I put a call out to Langley, and they were able to find heat signatures about forty feet underground in an old Soviet Era shelter about six miles southwest of where you nearly caught them on the river."

"You can find heat signatures from space?"

"We can do a lot of things," Topaz said. "The reason we don't always is that it carries some risk. Russia could easily have noticed our spy satellites scanning their territory. For all I know, they did and just decided not to say anything because they don't want to catch anymore flak for helping the Western imperialists. The point is, we have her. I'm sending you coordinates now."

He hung up, and Jake grinned at Jess. "I'm going after her."

"The hell you are," she said. "With one arm in a sling? Your trigger arm, no less?"

"I didn't say I was going alone. Call Munoz and have him wait downstairs for me with a vehicle. If Russia wants to have a problem with it, then they can talk to me. Or they can stop acting like cowards and help us."

"Okay, you said that, not me."

CHAPTER TWENTY THREE

The FSB either didn't care to follow up on the sudden American troop movement, or they did, and Topaz simply intercepted the call. The latter was more likely, since they weren't impeded in any way on their journey outside the city. In fact, the absence of a police response was so complete that Jake suspected Topaz was right, and the Russians were simply allowing the Secret Service to respond without interfering so that this diplomatic mess could be taken care of without them risking the wrath of their people by helping.

Not that Jake cared one way or another. He was going to rescue Sheila, and he didn't care who got the credit or who did the work. He just wanted her out of the clutches of that madman.

Munoz and his men were equally excited and equally focused. They leaned forward in their seats, their faces intense as they prepared to complete possibly the most important mission of their lives.

Actually, for most of them, this would be the second time they completed this mission. Back when this CAT was RRT Two, Munoz and most of the people present had assisted Jake in rescuing Sheila from Vincent St. Clair. Knowing that he had seasoned agents helping him increased Jake's confidence somewhat.

It would still have been nice to have his shooting arm.

The journey to the riverbend took them forty-five minutes. Jake resisted the urge to tell his men to move faster. The MRAPs were designed for protection, not speed.

When they finally did reach the riverbend, they stopped. "All right, Jake," Munoz said, "Where to?"

Jess spoke before Jake could ask the question. "Proceed west down that dirt road for eight miles, then south for six. The road parallels the river for a while. I would tell you to just drive straight across, but Topaz tells me the ground gets very rough and muddy, even for MRAPs, so it's faster to just take the road."

"Got it." He relayed that information to Munoz, and the vehicles continued down the road.

It took fifteen minutes for them to reach the turn. When they did, Munoz tapped his earpiece so everyone could hear. "We're going to come to a stop a mile before the entrance. Our CIA contact told me that it's a hatch with a ladder leading straight down. Mercer, do we have satellite feed?"

"Jess?"

"One second."

A moment later, Munoz nodded. "Confirmed. Okay, the President's daughter is being held seventy yards away from the entrance. So we're going to try to enter quietly, but if we encounter resistance, we're going to have to use frags."

One of the team members interrupted. "Do we worry they might kill the First Daughter if they know we're after her? Once they know, I mean?"

Munoz sighed. "Everything I've heard so far suggests no. They want her as leverage. That being said, be *very cautious* with use of force. The closer we can get the quieter we can get there, the better."

"Understood, sir."

Jake appreciated Munoz's caution. Intelligence suggested that Nikolai wouldn't kill her, but Nikolai's behavior had proven that he was a madman. Jake didn't trust that he would behave logically, especially if he found himself at risk.

They stopped nine minutes later, and the CAT checked their weapons. Jake checked his own handgun, fitted in a left-hand shoulder holster, and Munoz stopped him. "What do you think you're doing?"

"I'm coming with you."

"Jake, I appreciate where you're coming from, but you'll only slow us down. Don't take that the wrong way, it's just the way it is right now. You stay up top and give us sitreps."

"Jess will handle sitreps, and I won't slow you down. I'm going in."

Munoz's frown darkened, but he didn't argue. He knew Jake well enough to know that Jake wouldn't be dissuaded. "All right. In that case, you stay close to me. I really do appreciate your leadership, but you let me make the calls here. This is my wheelhouse, not yours."

"Understood." Realistically, Jake had far more combat experience than any of them, but he knew to quit while he was ahead.

The team disembarked and made their way to the compound. The team looked around, fingers on their triggers, each step calculated. They looked calm, but Jake knew they felt the same tension he did.

The enemy could be anywhere. They could be outside watching them right now. Drew could be sitting in a tree somewhere, his rifle poised to take them out before they even realized he was there.

When they reached the entrance, they breathed a collective sigh of relief. Temporary relief. They still had to clear the bunker of an unknown number of combatants.

Munoz held his hand for the team to stop. He tapped his earpiece and said quietly. "They're six feet from the entrance. Two guards. Frankie, drop down and disable them. One on either side. We'll follow once you confirm they're eliminated."

A wiry man of around thirty started forward. He lifted the hatch and jumped down without even bothering to use the ladder. Two seconds later, Jake heard a thump as he landed, then two coughs as his suppressed weapon eliminated the two guards.

"All clear."

The team wasted no time. Jake followed Munoz down the hatch, and the rest of the team came behind them. When everyone was gathered at the bottom, Munoz motioned to take the hallway to the left.

A voice called out in Russian, and Frankie leveled his rifle. When the Russian terrorist poked his head around the corner, Munoz fired, and the man dropped.

Then all hell broke loose. Jake heard shouting, and a moment later, half a dozen men began firing at them. The team dropped to the ground and Munoz tossed a flash bang. One of the terrorists rushed toward it, but Jake fired, and the man dropped just before the grenade went off. Jake and the CAT wore noise-canceling earpieces, and their goggles were set to cut off the visual feed for the flash, so the terrorists were the only ones to suffer from the explosion.

The CAT ensured that their suffering was short-lived.

Munoz tapped his earpiece. "We're going to descend a staircase in fifty feet, then we're going to reach the room where the President's daughter is held. I want precision, everyone. No stray shots that could hurt the President's daughter."

The ream proceeded forward, and when they reached the staircase, the hair on the back of Jake's neck stood up. "Behind!" he cried out.

Munoz and most of the CAT dropped to the ground automatically. Frankie was already opening the door and was a half-second behind. That half-second cost him his life when a volley of fire from behind them caught him in his chest.

"Dammit!" Munoz cried.

The team returned fire, but then more fire came from the stairwell, killing another agent.

"Shit! They're firing from both sides!"

Jake aimed carefully and fired. Another terrorist fell, and when one of his fellows turned his weapon to Jake, Munoz took him out. The team managed to hold off the terrorist pincer movement, but another agent fell as he was reloading.

"Jess, how many?"

"I don't know. The flash bang messed up the infrared."

Dammit. He hadn't thought of that.

"Munoz, infrared's down. We aren't sure how many."

"Doesn't matter," the seasoned Agent growled. "They'll all die today."

When a fourth agent fell to a terrorist bullet, though, Jake felt a touch of fear that maybe they didn't have enough.

"Fuck it," Munoz said. He pulled another flash-bang from his pocket. "If infrared's already down, then we might as well make things hard for these assholes."

He tossed the grenade ahead. The terrorists shouted and scrambled for cover.

The CAT was ready for them, and they smelled blood after losing four of their own. By the time Jake's visual feed kicked back on, all of the terrorists back the way they came were dead.

The team quickly stormed the stairwell. The terrorists here had been spared the worst of the blast, but they were still too disoriented to put up an effective resistance. Three terrorists fired on the team, all of whom missed, and then they were wiped out as well.

The team followed the stairwell to a heavy door with a ship's style wheel for a handle.

Jake pulled a grenade and commanded, "Everyone step back!"

"No!" Munoz barked. "We don't know if she's right behind that door."

Jake looked at the door and swore. He put the grenade back in his pocket and said, "Well then, what do we do?"

Munoz pulled out his flashlight and looked the door over. When his flashlight fell on the hinges, he said, "Okay. Here's the plan. We put small charges on the door hinges. Two of us hold the wheel and pull the door toward us once the charges go so it doesn't hurt anyone inside. Meanwhile, the rest have their weapons ready."

Jake nodded. "Okay. Let's get it done."

It took Munoz thirty seconds to set the small charges of plastic explosive on the door, but it felt like thirty hours to Jake. What if Sheila was killed while they were doing this?

He forced himself to stay calm, but it was the hardest thing he'd ever had to do.

"Okay," Munoz said. "Kaufman, help Mercer hold the door. On three... two... one..."

The charges went off with a loud pop. Jake and Kaufman pulled the door back and lifted it out of the way, letting it fall to the side with a resounding clang.

The team rushed into the room. It was empty.

Jake frowned. "I thought she was supposed to be here."

"Team, spread out," Munoz said. "Clear the room and look for the First Daughter."

The team spread out, kicking open doors to other rooms adjacent to the main room. Every few seconds, Jake heard them call, "Clear," as the rooms were confirmed empty of terrorists.

And of Sheila.

Jake's blood began to boil. Sheila was supposed to be here! Topaz had told him she would be here!

He tapped his earpiece and said, . "What the hell? Topaz? Are you there? Topaz?"

The voice that replied chilled Jake to the bone.

"I'm afraid that your friend is unable to come to the phone right now," Nikolai said. "But I'll tell you what you want to know. Sheila is not there. The heat signature you found was created by a small portable electric heater that I placed in the center of the room. It's unfortunate that I had to sacrifice so many of my loyal men, but of course, I didn't expect your assault team to be so effective. I rather hoped they would kill you. You continue to surprise me, Agent."

"Where is she?"

"She's back with her family." He chuckled. "Of course, her family doesn't know that yet."

"You're at the hotel?"

"I am. Along with an entire platoon of loyal Russian infantry, veterans of my security team who hope to return the Soviet Union to its rightful place of preeminence in the world."

"Jess," Jake said quickly. "They're in the hotel. Evacuate the President now!"

"Oh come, Agent. You surely don't believe I am that foolish? They can't hear you. They think you are embroiled in battle. Little do they know the battle will come to them. Besides, if they leave the building, your sniper friend will surely kill them."

Jake's eyes widened. "You're going to kill all of them. Not just the President."

"Of course not. I need your people angry. I need them to hate Russia. That way, they make the foolish decision to go to war."

"You're out of your mind. We'll flatten you in a war."

"With the proper leadership and the support of your allies, yes. I'm afraid that your allies will likely be quite unhappy with you when they learn it is your fault their heads of state have been massacred."

Jake shook his head in disbelief. "How do you plan to accomplish that?"

"I have more friends than you realize. There are soldiers in place at every hotel occupied by a foreigner. You cut the head off of a snake, the snake will die. The Western world is more like a hydra with many heads. I will cut all the heads off at once, and just like Hercules, I will burn them so they cannot grow back."

"Then what? We still outnumber and outgun Russia. Your nation will still lose."

"Perhaps. Or perhaps internal strife will tear you apart. I am not expecting Russia to destroy all of you. Simply to take its place as the world's next superpower."

A thought occurred to Jake. "Why are you telling me all of this?"

"I suppose I feel you deserve to know. You truly are a worthy opponent, Agent. A pity our interaction has to end so soon."

Jake frowned. So soon?

Then he realized. "Munoz! Get your team up top now!"

"Goodbye, Agent."

Jake sprinted to the hatch, the team close behind. He watched as the team ascended the ladder one by one. With his hurt arm, Jake went last. Munoz tossed a rope down to help him.

The seconds ticked by in Jake's mind as he ascended the ladder. Had it been thirty seconds since they left the room? Forty? How much time did they have? Was this just a bluff, or did Nikolai—

The ground heaved. Jake was thrown in the air and could only watch in horror as the team was engulfed in a ball of fire that shot from the tunnel. He curled into a ball but landed so heavily that the wind was knocked out of him. He lay on the ground, gasping as waves of pressure rolled over him.

CHAPTER TWENTY FOUR

"Jake! Jake! Mercer, wake up!"

Jake gasped and opened his eyes. Munoz was staring down at him. The CAT leader was bloody, and his uniform hung in tatters over his body. His body armor was intact, but shrapnel was embedded thickly in the armor plates.

"Come on," Munoz said, hauling Jake to his feet. "We have to go. The President's under attack."

The memory of his conversation with Nikolai came back to Jake. He nodded and said, "How many?"

"Six left," he said.

"Dammit."

"Could have been worse. We only lost three in the explosion. We can still crew both MRAPs."

The team split into three, and Jake followed Munoz to the front MRAP. The forest around them wasn't a forest anymore so much as it was a bomb crater. The bunker behind them was a crumbled ruin that was mostly aboveground, the majority of the ground having been blown away. The team scrambled over shattered rocks, piles of earth and fallen timbers as they headed back to the MRAPS.

The vehicles were parked barely three yards from the edge of the crater. They were covered in dirt, and the windshield on one of them was smashed, but when they climbed inside and started the engines, they powered up readily.

Thank God for small blessings.

As soon as he was in his seat, Jake tapped his earpiece. "Jess? God, please tell me you're here."

"I'm here," Jess replied. "I'm with the President and his family in the security room. We're holding the terrorists off in the lobby for now with help from Moscow Police, but it's not looking good. The enemy is very well trained. We've lost nearly sixty officers, and they're—Jake, they've reached the stairwell. Okay, Dawson, we need to evacuate."

"Don't," Jake said. "Drew's outside waiting for the President to show his face."

"Oh, *shit!* Jake, this is bad. We have no way out then."

"I know. We're coming to get you. Listen, this is important. Nikolai said Sheila is with them. I need eyes on Sheila and eyes on Drew ASAP."

"Can you get Topaz on the line? I haven't been able to get a hold of him either."

Jake sighed. "Topaz is dead. Nikolai got to him somehow."

"Shit!"

"Listen, he got to Topaz, but not Topaz's resources. Call Langley, tell them the situation, and get some imaging. It's the best chance we have right now."

"Okay. Please hurry, Jake."

"I will."

He tapped the earpiece and said, "Munoz, get us there ASAP. I don't give a damn what the hell you need to do. You can break the damned MRAP for all I care, but we need to be there yesterday."

"Understood. Here's hoping all those days of GTA helped."

"What's GTA?"

"It's a video game. Forget about it."

The team sped back to the hotel, but even at their best speed, they were thirty minutes out. Jake checked in with Jess every five minutes. The news wasn't encouraging. After twenty minutes, the terrorists had reached the President's suite.

"That's good news," Jake said. "They think he's still there. That will buy you some time."

"Yes, but three of our agents are there."

Jake sighed. "They might not be the only ones lost today."

"Is that supposed to encourage me?"

"No. Sorry. Listen, we're ten minutes out. You just need to hold out that long."

"Okay. Wait! Jake, I have Sheila!"

"You do?"

"Yes! She's on a rooftop across from the hotel's west face. Drew's with her, and so is someone I assume is Nikolai!"

"Get me the address. Munoz, I'm going after Sheila. I want your team to coordinate with Moscow Police and FSB and secure the President."

"You can't go by yourself."

"Keep the President safe."

Munoz frowned, but he didn't protest further. "Yes, sir."

When they neared the location, Jake heard a loud snap and saw a small crack on the windshield of the MRAP. Drew had seen them and fired on them.

"That's Drew. He's got a bead on us, so you need to be inside the building before you get out of the vehicles. Break into the parking garage if you have to. Good luck, Munoz."

Jake headed for the rear of the MRAP. Munoz slowed down to allow Jake time to jump out of the back and dash into the alley in between the building where Drew and Nikolai waited and another high-rise. Jake quickly ran to a fire escape and began to climb. If he injured his arm doing this, so be it.

Pain shot through his arm with each movement, but he gritted his teeth and forced himself higher. Sheila needed him.

He kept his eye on the roof, expecting Drew to poke his head over the top at any moment. Instead, he heard the heavy rattle of the M2, followed by cries from the roof. He tapped his earpiece. "Dammit, Munoz, Sheila's up here! Hold your fire!"

"Have a little faith, Jake," Munoz said. "I didn't hit her. I just bought you some time."

Jake reached the roof and rolled over. "Okay, well, hold your fire *now.*"

He stood up and leveled his handgun at the first person he saw.

The first person he saw was Nikolai.

The Russian Agent drew his pistol far faster than a man his age should have been able to move and pressed it against the head of the second person Jake saw.

Sheila turned to Jake, and her eyes widened in shock and hope. Nikolai yanked her out of the arms of the third person Jake saw and held her in front of him.

The third person Jake saw turned around, swinging his rifle toward Jake.

"No!" Nikolai commanded. "You watch for the President."

Drew ignored Nikolai and leveled his rifle at Jake. Jake quickly moved his weapon to cover Drew and said, "Don't make me do it, Drew. From this range, it's a kill shot, even with my left hand."

"Same to you, asshole," Drew snarled.

Jake looked into the hate-filled eyes of a man he once loved like a brother and searched for anything, any sign that he was still the man Jake thought he was. There must be some part of him that felt remorse for his actions, some little bit that could be redeemed.

137

But no. In those eyes, he saw only rage and hate and bitterness.

"No one will fire their weapons," Nikolai said calmly. "Or this time, I *will* kill her."

Sheila sobbed. "Oh, Jake. No, please."

"Hush, dear," Nikolai said. "Your man is resourceful, but he has made a fatal error coming alone. Agent, put your weapon down. We will not hurt you." He turned to Drew. "Will we?"

"Fuck that," Drew said, "I'm taking him out."

Jake fired. Drew caught his hands tightening on the trigger and dove to the side. The bullet struck his rifle instead. The bolt snapped off and flew over the side of the building, and Drew swore.

Jake turned his gun to Nikolai. He felt as though he was moving like molasses. He could see Nikolai's hand tighten on his own trigger. He fired, too quickly. The bullet struck Nikolai in the neck rather than the head. The Russian Agent spun around, firing as he did. The bullet cut a groove in Sheila's forehead but miraculously did no serious damage.

She screamed and pulled away from Nikolai, kicking the gun out of his reach.

Jake rushed toward her, covering Drew as he did. Drew glared at him, teeth bared, and lifted his hands.

Sheila threw her arms around Jake and sobbed with relief. God, just feeling her in his arms was payment enough for everything he had been through.

"Jake... Oh, Jake."

"You're all right," Jake said. "It's okay now. I need you to go find cover while I take care of these two."

"You might as well kill me," Drew snarled. "If you let me live, I won't stop."

Jake gently disengaged from Sheila, and she ran toward an HVAC unit and hid behind it, peeking around the corner to watch the confrontation unfold.

"Where's Bard?" Jake asked.

"Bard?" Drew spat. "Screw Bard. That coward gave up as soon as you landed Air Force One. He started drinking and moping about how he had tried his best and there was nothing he could do anymore. Dalton ran off to God knows where, and everyone else just scattered. Congratulations, Jake. You destroyed Trident."

138

Hearing that news would ordinarily fill Jake with joy, but Sheila was still in danger, and so was the President. Any congratulatory pats on the back would have to wait until later.

"So why are you here?" he asked Drew. "Why are you working with an enemy of the United States? You realize he's not trying to change the country; he's trying to overthrow it."

"Fuck the country!" Drew spat. "What has it ever done for me? For that matter, what has it ever done for you? We're just tools to them, Jake. Hell, everyone is. The politicians and presidents sit in their ivory towers and treat all of the normal people underneath them like animals. It's not going to change. It's never going to change. That's what Bard didn't understand. You can't just replace the leaders with new leaders because there will always be people coming up after you who just want to take and consume and use and don't care who gets caught up in it."

"And how are you helping people? When you stormed the White House and killed all of those agents, who did you help? When you protected Vincent St. Clair and he released a supervirus in Paris that killed thousands, who benefited? When you gave Hadad information that he used to destroy the Western Wall, killing hundreds, what cause did you serve?"

"*My* cause, idiot! That's all anyone can do is help themselves. You can't count on governments." He sneered. "Or friends."

"And did you not say that it was Staff Sergeant McNeill's suggestion that you abandon your comrades to enemy fire and instead engage the rear guard of the terrorist column?"

"That wasn't... no, I—"

"You did not say that?"

Jake blinked, trying to figure out how this had gone so wrong so fast. This wasn't what he was trying to say, damn it! They'd had no choice!

"We both agreed that—"

"But it was Staff Sergeant McNeill's suggestion that you agreed with, wasn't it, Staff Sergeant Mercer?"

"You're not listening!"

"Answer the question, Staff Sergeant!"

"Yes! God damn it, yes! But it's not—"

"No further questions."

Jake looked at his former friend, a tear in his eye. "Drew... that wasn't my fault. I didn't know that they were going to use my

139

testimony against you. They told me they were going to clear both of us."

"Then you're stupid. That's worth punishment too. You threw me under the bus, and you can talk all day about what you *meant* to do or what you *wanted* to happen. That's what happened, Jake. I was made a scapegoat because of *you*.

"Except when I thought about it, it wasn't really because of you. Like me, you were just a tool they used. That's why I'm coming after them. After *him*. There's no cause, Jake. There's no purpose. I'm just getting them back."

He chuckled bitterly. "You got me. And I'm sure that your team down there will make short work of Nikolai's boys. We won't kill the President. We won't kill Sheila either. You win. Just like you always do. But I won too. I made an impression on the world. I showed what one person can do when he's fucking angry. I showed what can happen when all of the angry people in the world who are taken advantage of by the assholes in power who see them as nothing more than cattle rise up and fight back. Look down there, Jake. Tell me what you see."

Jake looked down and saw bursts of gunfire inside the hotel. He saw dozens of police officers surrounding the building, weapons drawn.

And he saw civilians pouring out of their homes and businesses, rushing the officers, throwing rocks and debris, shouting and singing the Soviet anthem. He saw them smash the windows of police cars, and as he watched, a flaming bottle flew through the air and lit one of the police vehicles on fire.

"That's right," Drew said. "You see small people fed up at being used as doormats by big people. And you know what? They're going to win. The people in charge on all sides of whatever war they have you brainwashed into believing is going on are going to realize that their tools aren't working anymore. They're going to either fight and die, or they're going to give in and be forced to acknowledge the rights of everyone to be heard and to be listened to."

"You're out of your mind, Drew. You're not a Messiah. You're a murderer. You've killed thousands of those people you claim to be trying to save."

"I'm not trying to save them. That's what you'd call an ancillary benefit." He grinned. "I'm trying to kill you."

"Jake!"

140

Jake turned to Sheila. He caught movement out of the corner of his eye. Nikolai had reached his weapon and now lifted it toward Jake. Jake lifted his own weapon, but he wouldn't reach Nikolai in time.

Jake heard Sheila cry, and a moment later, a heavy lead bar hit Nikolai in the head. Nikolai fell to the ground with a gasp. Jake looked at the lead bar. It appeared to be some sort of breaker bar to remove heavy bolts. He looked at Sheila, who said, "I found it on the floor. I... Jake! Behind you!"

He turned around and saw Drew aiming a hideaway handgun at his head. Jake rolled over, and the bullet meant for his head hit the roof. He aimed at Drew and fired. Once more, the shot missed its mark. It hit Drew in the chest instead of the head.

Drew's body armor caught it, but the terrorist was unbalanced. The slug pushed him backward. His heel caught on the rail, and he fell backward over the roof.

The last thing Jake saw of him was his eyes growing wide as he realized what was about to happen. Then he heard a piercing shriek as his one-time friend fell nine stories to his death.

Jake's chest burned, and each breath came with an effort. Drew's last shot had punctured his lung. He got to his feet and stumbled over to Nikolai. He tried to lift his handgun, but when he saw blood flowing from the side of Nikolai's head and a red stain blooming on his shirt, he let his handgun drop.

He collapsed to his knees next to the Russian Agent. Nikolai turned his eyes up to him and grinned. "Checkmate."

"Whatever you say," Jake gasped.

Nikolai laughed. Then he stilled.

Jess's voice came over Jake's earpiece. "Jake, it's Jess. The terrorists are defeated. The President is safe."

Jake nodded. His vision swam. "'S'okay. It's over now. Sheila..."

"Jake!" She rushed to him. "Please don't die! Please! Our baby needs you!"

His eyes widened. "Baby? Sheila, that's..."

He wasn't sure if he finished his sentence or not before he fell into darkness.

EPILOGUE

"You're sure about this, huh?"

Jake nodded. "I'm sure. It's time."

"Bard's still out there, you know."

Jess's words brought a pang of guilt to Jake. "Yes. I know. Before he died, Drew told me that Bard had given up, but I know he'll probably be back eventually."

"You don't want to stick around so you can be there when he returns? Or at least until Bryan leaves office?"

Jake sighed and shook his head. "No. It's time. I've been running from this for a while, but I think I made my decision the moment I saw Sheila in St. Clair's grasp."

Jess nodded. Tears came to her eyes, and she blinked them away. "Well, I can't say I didn't see it coming. I'm not going to pretend to be happy about it, though."

He chuckled. "I know. I don't expect you to be."

The two of them sat on the patio of Fred's Hoagies, the best sandwich shop in Washington, D.C. Jake had finally been released from the hospital after a month of convalescence. He had lost, according to the doctor, nearly ninety percent of the blood in his body. It was a miracle he had survived.

Jake was done relying on miracles. As soon as he left the hospital, he told Art that he was retiring from the Secret Service, effective immediately.

Art had tried to talk him out of it, rather more vehemently than Sheila. He pointed out that Jake was his best Agent, that the President owed him his life, that he would never find anyone able to do what Jake could do. Jake listened patiently, but his mind was made up.

"Don't worry, Art. If we're being honest, Jess's intelligence was at least as crucial to our success, if not more so. As far as fighting goes, I didn't do as well as you think I did. Well, sometimes, I did, but Garrett's RRT had to save my ass a couple times, and Munoz had to pick up where she left off. You'll find other agents who can do the job, and most importantly, you'll find other agents who can do it without allowing themselves to become compromised."

142

Art had finally acquiesced on that last point. When he shook Jake's hand, he made it clear that Jake always had a job with the Secret Service if he wanted to return.

Jake thanked him, but he knew he wouldn't return. The stakes had finally gotten too high for him to ignore.

Jess guessed at that reason with her next statement. "It's because of the baby, isn't it?"

Jake nodded. "Yes. I promised Sheila that I wouldn't put myself in danger anymore for the sake of our child. In return, she had to promise the same thing."

"So no more following Daddy to dangerous 'peace' summits?"

"No more following Daddy."

She nodded, and a tear fell from her eyes. "When did you two find out?"

"When she was in the hospital, the doctor noticed that she had two heartbeats. Turns out one of the heartbeats wasn't hers."

"That's cute. How did Jess take it?"

"Well, she made me promise to quit, and then she made an immediate appointment for new teeth."

"How did that go, by the way?"

"Well, she couldn't take general anesthetic because of the pregnancy, so they pumped her full of enough novocaine that I'm pretty sure she's still laughing."

Jess giggled. "I mean the teeth. They look okay?"

He nodded. "They're beautiful, but I'm just glad she's safe. I told her I wouldn't care if she was toothless. I'd love her anyway."

"So you learned your first lesson as an engaged man. Good for you."

He grimaced. "Yeah, I won't make that mistake again."

"What about the ring? Still upset that it's on her right hand?"

His mile faded slightly. "She's handling it better than me. Let's just say it's one more reason I'm glad it's over."

"Yeah, I understand that." She smiled, and there was joy mixed with her sadness. She met Jake's eyes and said, "I'm happy for you two. I really am. I just…" her lower lip trembled. "I just wish you guys didn't have to move away."

Jake smiled. "Well, that's some good news for you."

Her eyes popped open. "You're not moving away?"

He shook his head. "No. Bryan's giving me a job as White House Security Consultant. No carrying guns or protecting VIPs, but I'll be advising the Office of Management and Budget and the White House Chief of Staff on security needs. I'll still get to annoy Art, but this time it will be when I tell him that OMB is whining about the Secret Service's training expenses."

Jess jumped up and threw her arms around Jake. He winced. "Ouch. Careful. Shoulder and lung still hurt."

"I don't care. You can deal with it for leaving me."

"Hey, I'm not going anywhere. Haven't you been listening? We can still have sandwiches and movie nights, and Art's going to let me use the training facility, so I can keep kicking your ass when you feel a need for punishment. Ow! Okay, that's not fair. I'm injured."

She giggled and released his wrist. He rubbed it and glared at her. "Taking advantage of a sick, old man. For shame."

"Oh, whatever. You deserve it."

"Yeah." He chuckled. "I know."

"So when is little Jess due?"

Jake laughed. "If I named my kid after you, you'd smack me over the head and tell me to change it immediately."

"Yeah, probably. Besides, Carrie's a good name. Even if she hated you."

Jake's smile faded. "I don't think she ever hated me. I think she just hated what I represented."

"Protection and safety?"

"The need for protection and safety." He fell quiet a moment, then said. "It sucks, you know? All most people want is to just live their lives peacefully and in comfort. They don't need great wealth or great power or even fame and success. They just want to enjoy the time they have without wondering when some asshole with a rifle is going to slaughter them and their families for no good reason. People like you and me, we assume that risk. We know that we might end up dead one day. Bryan assumed that risk, too, but he assumed it *for* Carrie and Sheila. They didn't get a choice. When Sheila fell in love with me and not a nice doctor or lawyer somewhere in Small Town America, I think it took away Carrie's hope that there would be an end to that risk one day. If I could change anything, I would go back and get her home safely so that she could escape the way Sheila did."

Jess reached forward and laid her hand over Jake's. "You did good, Jake. You did the best you could. That's all anyone can ask, and more than most people do. And don't listen to me and Art. You've earned your retirement. Forget about the news and the fighting and the strife.

One thing Nikolai didn't consider is exactly what you said. Most people don't want to fight and die, and as time goes on, fewer and fewer people do. We're slow learners, we humans, but at least we aren't stoppers."

Jake nodded. "That's true. Slowly but surely, we keep moving forward."

"Amen to that."

Jake's phone buzzed. "That's Sheila. I'll call you—"

"You will do no such thing. You will enjoy a nice, peaceful evening with your fiancé, and for the next twenty-four hours, you will forget all about me, the President, the Secret Service, and everything else but your family. You got that, buster?"

He smiled. "I got it."

"Good. Now go get a piece of that First Daughter ass."

He rolled his eyes. "Never change, Jess."

"Hell no. Why would I do that?"

Jake paid for his meal and headed home. Sheila had grudgingly allowed him to keep riding his motorcycle, but that didn't mean she wouldn't give him grief about it. When he arrived home, he found her standing in front of their new house with her hands on her hips.

"Did you ride that fast the whole way here? For God's sake, Jake, you're going to be a father. You can't—"

Jake pulled her into his arms and kissed her deeply. She gasped and stiffened briefly, then melted into his arms. When he pulled away, he stared down into her bright, fathomless blue eyes. "I love you."

She giggled. "I love you too. Where did that come from?"

He shrugged. "Just looking forward to the rest of our lives."

"Me too. I can't wait—Ooh!"

He swept her off her feet and kissed her again. Then he carried her across the threshold.

The door closed behind him, and Jake and Sheila entered the first night of the rest of their lives.

NOW AVAILABLE!

ABSOLUTE VENGEANCE
(A Jake Mercer Political Thriller—Book #6)

"Thriller writing at its best."
--Midwest Book Review (*Any Means Necessary*)

From the #1 bestselling and USA Today bestselling author Jack Mars (with over 10,000 five-star reviews) comes a groundbreaking new political thriller series: when the President of the United States or his family are threatened, it is up to Jake Mercer, former Marine sniper turned Secret Service agent, to protect them from dangers—both foreign and domestic.

When the President's motorcade is ambushed by a rogue drone strike, Secret Service Agent Jake Mercer is thrust into a lethal game of cat and mouse. With the nation's leader in his charge, will Mercer's wit be enough to save the leader of the free world?

"Thriller enthusiasts who relish the precise execution of an international thriller, but who seek the psychological depth and believability of a protagonist who simultaneously fields professional and personal life challenges, will find this a gripping story that's hard to put down."
--Midwest Book Review, Diane Donovan (regarding Any Means Necessary)

"One of the best thrillers I have read this year. The plot is intelligent and will keep you hooked from the beginning. The author did a superb job creating a set of characters who are fully developed and very much enjoyable. I can hardly wait for the sequel."
--Books and Movie Reviews, Roberto Mattos (re Any Means Necessary)

ABSOLUTE VENGEANCE is the sixth book in a new series by #1 bestselling and critically acclaimed author Jack Mars, whose books have received over 10,000 five-star reviews and ratings. The series begins with ABSOLUTE THREAT (book #1).

A gripping and unpredictable political thriller, the Jake Mercer series is a page-turning action series that will leave you unable to put it down. This fresh and exciting action hero will have you turning pages late into the night, and fans of Brad Taylor, Vince Flynn, and Tom Clancy are sure to fall in love.

Future books in the series are also available!

Jack Mars

Jack Mars is the USA Today bestselling author of the LUKE STONE thriller series, which includes seven books. He is also the author of the new FORGING OF LUKE STONE prequel series, comprising six books; of the AGENT ZERO spy thriller series, comprising twelve books; of the TROY STARK thriller series, comprising eight books; of the SPY GAME thriller series, comprising ten books; of the JAKE MERCER thriller series, comprising seven books (and counting); of the TYLER WOLF thriller series, comprising seven books (and counting); and of the new LARA KING thriller series, comprising seven books (and counting).

Jack loves to hear from you, so please feel free to visit www.Jackmarsauthor.com to join the email list, receive a free book, receive free giveaways, connect on Facebook and Twitter, and stay in touch!

BOOKS BY JACK MARS

LARA KING THRILLER SERIES
ASSET ONE (Book #1)
ASSET TWO (Book #2)
ASSET THREE (Book #3)
ASSET FOUR (Book #4)
ASSET FIVE (Book #5)
ASSET SIX (Book #6)
ASSET SEVEN (Book #7)

TYLER WOLF THRILLER SERIES
DOUBLE AGENT (Book #1)
DOUBLE CROSS (Book #2)
DOUBLE ASSET (Book #3)
DOUBLE DOCTRINE (Book #4)
DOUBLE JEOPARDY (Book #5)
DOUBLE THREAT (Book #6)
DOUBLE TARGET (Book #7)

JAKE MERCER THRILLER SERIES
ABSOLUTE THREAT (Book #1)
ABSOLUTE DAMAGE (Book #2)
ABSOLUTE FORCE (Book #3)
ABSOLUTE PERIL (Book #4)
ABSOLUTE TREASON (Book #5)
ABSOLUTE VENGEANCE (Book #6)
ABSOLUTE TARGET (Book #7)

THE SPY GAME
TARGET ONE (Book #1)
TARGET TWO (Book #2)
TARGET THREE (Book #3)
TARGET FOUR (Book #4)
TARGET FIVE (Book #5)
TARGET SIX (Book #6)
TARGET SEVEN (Book #7)
TARGET EIGHT (Book #8)

TARGET NINE (Book #9)
TARGET TEN (Book #10)

TROY STARK THRILLER SERIES
ROGUE FORCE (Book #1)
ROGUE COMMAND (Book #2)
ROGUE TARGET (Book #3)
ROGUE MISSION (Book #4)
ROGUE SHOT (Book #5)
ROGUE STRIKE (Book #6)
ROGUE ORDER (Book #7)
ROGUE ATTACK (Book #8)

LUKE STONE THRILLER SERIES
ANY MEANS NECESSARY (Book #1)
OATH OF OFFICE (Book #2)
SITUATION ROOM (Book #3)
OPPOSE ANY FOE (Book #4)
PRESIDENT ELECT (Book #5)
OUR SACRED HONOR (Book #6)
HOUSE DIVIDED (Book #7)

FORGING OF LUKE STONE PREQUEL SERIES
PRIMARY TARGET (Book #1)
PRIMARY COMMAND (Book #2)
PRIMARY THREAT (Book #3)
PRIMARY GLORY (Book #4)
PRIMARY VALOR (Book #5)
PRIMARY DUTY (Book #6)

AN AGENT ZERO SPY THRILLER SERIES
AGENT ZERO (Book #1)
TARGET ZERO (Book #2)
HUNTING ZERO (Book #3)
TRAPPING ZERO (Book #4)
FILE ZERO (Book #5)
RECALL ZERO (Book #6)
ASSASSIN ZERO (Book #7)
DECOY ZERO (Book #8)
CHASING ZERO (Book #9)

Made in the USA
Coppell, TX
12 August 2024

35872035R00094